Conner's heart was pounding as he played, and he could barely believe he was getting the words out. Elizabeth's gaze never wavered. She didn't look away in embarrassment. She didn't fake a cough so she could avert her eyes. She might have been breathing a little heavier, but she wasn't going to let him win.

As the last chord faded away, Conner felt himself coming down from an incredible high. Elizabeth had never looked as beautiful as she did at that moment—all flushed and glassy-eyed in the soft light. He had never wanted to be alone with anyone so badly.

Francine Pascal's SVH senioryear

So Cool

CREATED BY
FRANCINE PASCAL

BANTAM BOOKS
NEW YORK · TORONTO · LONDON · SYDNEY · AUCKLAND

RL 6, age 12 and up

SO COOL

A Bantam Book / April 1999

17th
Street
Productions
A Division of Daniel Weiss Associates, Inc.

Produced by 17th Street Productions,
a division of Daniel Weiss Associates, Inc.
33 West 17th Street
New York, NY 10011.

ISBN: 0-553-57028-5

Published simultaneously in the United States and Canada

*Bantam Books are published by Bantam Books, a division of Random
House, Inc. Its trademark, consisting of the words "Bantam Books" and
the portrayal of a rooster, is Registered in U.S. Patent and Trademark
Office and in other countries. Marca Registrada. Bantam Books, 1540
Broadway, New York, New York 10036.*

PRINTED IN THE UNITED STATES OF AMERICA

OPM   0 9 8 7 6 5 4 3 2 1

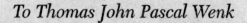

To Thomas John Pascal Wenk

Conner McDermott

I don't have a single decent song. After writing lyrics and playing the guitar my entire life, I don't have one song I would sing in public. It's pathetic.

What brought this revelation on? Gavin, my guitar teacher, hooked me up with a gig. A real gig at House of Java, where there will be a lot of people. People who'll expect me to be some kind of Clapton-Hendrix hybrid because they know I've been taking lessons for years and practicing all the time.

So I'm going onstage and I have nothing to play. Ironic, since I have enough going on in my life to fill a dozen volumes of alternative angst rock. But unlike all those Eddie Vedder disciples out there, I'm not stupid. I don't actually believe anyone cares enough to listen.

Jessica Wakefield

It was bad enough when they wrote "Jessica Wakefield is a slut" on the blackboard. Bad enough? It was horrible. But I figured there was just a rumor circulating that I'd rounded the bases with Will. It's not true, but it's the kind of thing people don't talk about for very long. I had even started to think that Liz was right — that everything would blow over as soon as someone else . . . rounded the bases.

But the things they're saying about me are a lot worse than that. They're the kinds of things that make people ask to hear the story again, that make people repeat the story and add to it and blow it up until it's so big, no one can forget.

And sometimes, even the people who made the stories up start believing them.

Elizabeth Wakefield

Maria thinks I should get to know Conner better. She thinks if I "know him the way she does," I'll learn to like him.

What she doesn't know is that I'd love to know more about Conner. I'd love to know what Tia meant when she said he was "complicated." I'd love to know why he wandered into my room on Friday night all apologetic and morose. I'd love to know if he was really going to kiss me when he leaned over my bed or if I just imagined it.

But one thing's for sure—Maria doesn't know him as well as she thinks she does. I don't think anyone <u>really</u> knows him.

And I think he likes it that way.

Conner let the final chord of his new song fade into the air, then placed his hands over the strings to silence them. He paused a moment and adopted a poker face. No point in looking hopeful.

"So?" Conner asked Tia Ramirez, his best friend and most honest critic.

Tia placed her hands on the knees of her beat-up jeans and pushed herself up from the couch. She shuffled across Conner's bedroom with her arms folded and her eyes down.

Conner swallowed with difficulty. "It sucked, right? It's a Manilow."

"I wouldn't say it was a *Manilow*," Tia answered. She finally looked up, and her brown eyes were sparkling. "It was great, Conner. Really excellent."

Conner grinned and flung his pick at her. "Thanks, loser." He bit his lip and looked at the floor. "You really think it was decent?"

"Yeah." Tia walked over to his stereo, picked up an old vinyl album from the stack in the corner, and studied it. "I mean, you might want to work on your transitions a little—"

"Yeah, they're a little rusty," Conner said, running a hand through his hair. Should he tell her?

"And some of the high notes are a little flat—"

"Uh-huh." His leg started to bounce.

"But other than that—"

Conner closed his eyes. "Tia, I have a gig," he blurted out, leaning forward on his bed.

"Say that again," Tia said.

"So what I really want to know is—," Conner said, staring at the floor. "Is that song decent enough to play in public?"

"You have a gig?" Tia dropped the album.

"Yeah. At House of Java this week." Conner laid his guitar down on the bed next to him and stood, wiping his palms on his jeans. Tia's look of delighted surprise was already making him regret opening his mouth.

"Conner! That's amazing!" she said, rushing across the room and jumping into his arms. Conner almost fell back onto the bed. "This week? Why didn't you tell me sooner?"

Conner shrugged her off. "It's no big deal. I just kind of fell into it."

"No big deal? Are you kidding? Are they paying you?"

"Yeah. But not all that much."

"Doesn't matter. If they're paying you, you're a

2

professional," Tia said. Her eyes widened. "A *professional!*"

"Shhh!" Conner grabbed her hands. "Megan
doesn't know yet."

"Why not?" Tia asked.

"Because." *Because she'd make a big deal out of
it like you are right now.*

"Ooookay." Tia rolled her eyes, but lowered her
voice. "Conner, this could be your big break, you
know? Like, someone hears you and next thing
you're number one on the charts! CDs! Music
videos!"

Okay, Tia was blowing this thing way out of
proportion. Sure, maybe he was a little bit psyched
about the gig, but it was just a stupid coffeehouse.
"Hey, slow down," he said, pulling his hands out of
Tia's. "It's a onetime deal. They needed acts and I
was there, that's all."

"Well, I think it's awesome," Tia said.

Conner sat down again and fiddled with the
neck of his guitar. If he hadn't told her, he could
still back out and not let anyone down. Now Tia
was all excited, and she'd never understand if
Conner decided to scrap the whole idea. He'd just
cut his options down to none.

"What's the matter, Conner?" Tia asked. "Are
you afraid no one will come?"

No, he was afraid they'd come and think he
was rank. "Gimme a break, Tee," he said.

"Well, don't worry about it, because I have an idea," Tia said, starting to pace.

"Hey, would you stop moving for a second?" Conner protested as Tia practically burned a trail into his rug.

True to form, Tia totally ignored him. "If we get a ton of people to show, the manager will ask you back, right?"

"What do you mean, 'we'?" Conner asked. The walls seemed to be closing in. The buzz of his old amp started to grate on his nerves, so he flicked it off.

"We can get everyone we know to come and make them tell everyone *they* know," Tia continued. Her eyes were glazing over in a way that made Conner more than a little nervous. "When the manager sees the crowd you draw, he'll want you to come back, which will obviously kill the onetime-gig bit. Naturally once that happens, we ask for more money and a percentage of the gross—"

"Hey, hey, hey!" Conner interrupted her with a violent wave of his arms. "I told you this was no big deal, and I meant it. I appreciate the sentiment, Tia, but you're not my manager, okay?"

"Oh, yeah?" Tia said, all five feet of her totally in his face. "Well, maybe I should be."

Conner fell back onto his bed and placed his

hands over his eyes. This was going to be one very long week.

"So, what's going on with you girls?" Mr. Wakefield asked, leaning his elbows on the football-shaped table at First and Ten. "Any good gossip to report?"

Elizabeth Wakefield laughed. "Dad! Gossip?"

"Well, we decided to have this once-a-week family dinner to catch up with each other, right?" Mrs. Wakefield said.

"Right," Elizabeth said as she took a sip of water and put her glass on her paper baseball-trivia place mat. "But can Jessica and I have a say in where we go next time?"

"You don't like this place?" Mr. Wakefield asked.

Elizabeth glanced around the restaurant. There were at least eight televisions hanging from the ceiling around the bar in the front of the room, each showing a different sporting event. Cheers and boos erupted from the crowd about every five seconds, and the bartender rang a cowbell each time someone scored. Every wall was covered with sports memorabilia, from autographed baseball caps, to Olympic swimming goggles, to a pair of giant sneakers that once belonged to some basketball player. There was a football game on the huge television in the back, and two men were arguing over which team would win.

"It's a little . . . loud?" Elizabeth said as the cowbell rang again.

"Yeah. And too many people from school work here," Jessica muttered, sliding down slightly in her seat.

"Like who?" Mrs. Wakefield asked, glancing at a passing waitress.

"Mom, you know Maria Slater works here," Elizabeth said. "You were there when she came over all psyched about the job."

"Well, I'd say if your best friend works here, it's good enough for you to eat here," Mr. Wakefield said.

Jessica glanced at Elizabeth and rolled her eyes. Apparently that subject was closed.

"So, Elizabeth," Mrs. Wakefield said, leaning back in her chair. "Tell us about Conner McDermott."

Elizabeth nearly spit her water across the table. She reached for a napkin, wiped her mouth, and swallowed.

"What do you want to know?" Elizabeth asked. She shot her sister a pleading look, but Jessica was too busy not eating her salad to notice.

"You're living in the same house with this boy and we never met him," Mrs. Wakefield said, tugging at her pearls. "Do you get along?"

"Sure!" Elizabeth chirped. Like oil and water. "Conner's great. He's very . . . smart." It wasn't a lie, but it also wasn't the first word that came to mind. *Gorgeous. Guarded. Mysterious. Complicated.* But she didn't want her parents to think she was living with some seductive soap-opera character.

"Well, if you two are friends, we'd like to meet him," Elizabeth's father put in.

"I wouldn't say we're friends, exactly," Elizabeth hedged. She had no idea what she and Conner were, but she was sure they were something her parents wouldn't understand.

"Hi, Wakefields!"

Elizabeth looked up to find Maria hovering over the table.

"Hey. Didn't your shift end over an hour ago?" Elizabeth asked. One thing she'd neglected to tell her parents was that Maria and Conner were seeing each other. It was a small fact she preferred to ignore as much as possible.

"I stayed late to cover for Jade," Maria said. She was wearing a referee's shirt, a baseball cap over her short, black curls, and that isn't-life-fabulous grin she'd been sporting lately. "I'm outta here now, though."

"Can you join us?" Mrs. Wakefield asked.

Maria glanced at the door. "Thanks, but Conner should be here any minute."

Elizabeth's heart did a bungee jump to her stomach.

"Conner?" Mrs. Wakefield looked at Elizabeth. "I thought you said you two weren't friends."

Maria's face turned stony, but she cleared it quickly. "Liz and Conner aren't exactly a match made in heaven," Maria said, meeting Elizabeth's eye. "But they'll learn to love each other soon if I have anything to say about it."

Elizabeth couldn't even begin to respond to that one, so she stuffed a huge forkful of salad into her mouth and chewed. But she found she was so panicked by the idea of seeing Conner, she couldn't swallow. She'd avoided him for most of the weekend—ever since he almost kissed her. Maybe.

"There he is!" Maria said. "Conner! Over here!"

Elizabeth's insides snaked into a coil as the whole family turned to look. Even Jessica, who'd barely moved in the last fifteen minutes, took a peek.

"He's adorable!" Mrs. Wakefield gushed. Elizabeth forced her food down in a painful lump.

"Mom!" she hissed.

"Isn't he, though?" Maria added. That grin again.

"Seriously, Maria," Jessica said, riveted. "That guy is total eye candy."

"Don't get any ideas, Jess," Maria warned.

Oh, please! Elizabeth thought as Mr. Adorable approached the table.

"Hey," Conner said, reaching out and entwining his fingers with Maria's. Elizabeth felt sick as his green eyes focused admiringly on her best friend. She couldn't help remembering how intensely those eyes had looked at her just two nights ago. But it didn't matter. He was with Maria. *Just introduce him and go,* Elizabeth thought.

"Oh, shoot," Maria said. "I forgot to punch out. Be right back." She pecked Conner quickly on the cheek before rushing toward the back of the restaurant.

Oh, no. Elizabeth fought the urge to slide out of her chair and hide under the table. Conner was staring at his boots as her family looked at her expectantly. Unfortunately, her power of speech was AWOL.

Mrs. Wakefield's eyes darted from Conner to Elizabeth and back again. "Well, Conner, we were just talking about you."

Could she have possibly picked a worse thing to say? Elizabeth hoped First and Ten's dim lights would hide her flaming cheeks.

Conner cleared his throat. "Really?" he asked. He wiped his hands on the seat of his jeans and lifted an eyebrow in Elizabeth's direction.

Elizabeth straightened up. This was no big

9

deal. *He* was no big deal. "Mom, Dad, Jessica, this is Conner Decmermott." *Oh God.* "I mean McDermott."

Conner smirked, then shook everyone's hand. "Nice to finally meet you," he said to Jessica, flashing a charming smile just as Maria returned.

"You too." Jessica smiled back. It was small, but it was the first smile Elizabeth had seen on her all evening. Practically the first words she'd spoken.

"Well," Maria said, grabbing Conner's hand again. "Let's leave the Wakefields to their quality time."

"Sure," Conner replied. "Nice meeting you all." He held Elizabeth's gaze for a split second before allowing Maria to lead him out by the hand.

Mr. Wakefield nodded at the departing couple. "He seems like a nice guy," he said.

"Yes. A little quiet, but nice," Mrs. Wakefield agreed. "What is it you don't like about him, Elizabeth?"

"Yeah, you should have snagged him for yourself," Jessica added, suddenly looking animated. "He's a total babe."

Elizabeth closed her eyes and counted to ten. Yep, nothing like an old-fashioned family dinner to start the week off right.

"You were quiet tonight, Jess," Mrs. Wakefield remarked, turning around in the front passenger's seat as they drove back to the Fowlers' after dinner. "Everything okay?"

Jessica sighed, her eyes locked on the fleeting silhouettes of the houses and trees at the side of the road. "I've got a lot on my mind, I guess. You know, there's that twentieth-century history exam coming up," she said. "And I'm kind of tired," she added, hoping her mother wouldn't delve any deeper.

"Well, I'm glad you're finally focusing on your schoolwork, Jess," Mrs. Wakefield said with a smile. Jessica let out a breath of relief when her mother settled back in her seat and began to chat with Jessica's father.

She would have leaned back and closed her eyes, but every time she did, she saw the scene that had played out at the Riot on Friday night—Lila and Amy, her two best friends, turning their backs on her as Melissa Fox and her El Carro buddies mocked her.

Mr. Wakefield pulled into the Fowlers' driveway, and Jessica was the first out of the car. Lila had made herself scarce all weekend. If Jessica was going to talk to her and find out what was going on before school tomorrow, this was her last chance.

Jessica rushed inside and started up the spiral staircase, her heart in her throat. Halfway up, she heard a door open on the second floor. A moment

11

later Lila stood on the landing in front of her.

They stared at each other a moment, then Lila turned and headed back toward her room.

"Lila!" Jessica called, taking the rest of the steps two at a time. "Can you just stop for a second?"

Lila paused in front of her door, but didn't turn around. "I'm really busy."

"I want you to tell me what's going on," Jessica said. Her hands were shaking, so she stuffed them under her arms. "Why did you and Amy do that to me?"

Lila let out an exasperated breath and faced Jessica. "You have no idea?"

"No, I don't." Jessica hated the plea in her voice, but she couldn't hide it. "How could you stab me in the back like that?"

"You stabbed Melissa in the back," Lila said simply, as if it were the most obvious answer in the world.

"What?" Jessica said. "Are you kidding me? I didn't even know she and Will were together! And she wasn't even my friend! You're *my* best friend. How can you side with a total stranger over me?"

Lila's brown eyes were hard. "I just want to be popular by association, remember?" she said. Jessica's stomach turned. During an argument the week before, Jessica had accused Lila of riding Melissa's coattails to popularity. When was she going to learn to keep her mouth shut?

"Look, Jess, it's not my fault," Lila continued. "Melissa's a nice person. And you tried to steal her boyfriend and then rub her face in it. You're always doing stuff like that, and this time it backfired on you."

"I can't believe you're saying this to me!" Jessica said, tears spilling over onto her cheeks.

Lila shook her head and rolled her eyes. "God, Jess. Why do you always have to be so dramatic about everything?" As Lila brushed past her, Jessica fought the urge to reach out and push the girl down the stairs. She had seen Lila's harsh, elitist, obnoxious side in the past, but she never thought it would turn against her.

One more of Jessica's worst nightmares had come true.

Jessica Wakefield

I used to love being a beautiful blonde. I know I sound conceited, but bear with me. I was obsessive about my appearance — always wearing trendy clothes and makeup, my hair long and healthy, enhanced with highlights. It got me a lot of attention, especially from guys.

But there's a downside to looking that way that I never realized before. One wrong word whispered in the right ears and it all turns against you. What used to be sexy is cheap. The short, tight clothes aren't flirtatious — they're slutty. The label of "party girl" takes on a whole different meaning. One I'd rather not mention.

I used to think Liz was crazy, dressing so

conservatively, never bothering to pick up a fashion magazine. But I can't help thinking that if the rumors everyone has been spreading about me had been started about Liz, they never would have taken hold. She just doesn't look the part. Or act it. Dating around is not Elizabeth's thing, but I've always accepted dates from practically everyone who asked. I mean, how are you supposed to find <u>the</u> <u>one</u> if you don't go out with lots of people? But if I'd known how easily that could turn on me, I never would have done it.

I hate people looking at me now, especially guys. I know what they're thinking.

Maybe if I blend into the crowd, they'll eventually forget I'm even there.

Elizabeth Wakefield

My favorite books are novels where people rise above the ordinary and do something wonderful—you know, the kind where a character will put himself in peril to save a total stranger.

The characters aren't perfect. They're real people who sometimes mess up. But in the end they always come through, overcoming their weaknesses to do what their hearts tell them is right.

I've always identified with those characters. I always thought I'd be selfless and noble too if I were in their situation. But I'm beginning to realize that thinking you'd do something and doing it are two entirely different things.

In creative writing class, Mr. Quigley

is always saying, "Write what you know—
use your own feelings, your own
experiences, to make your characters
real." I've been trying, but to tell the
truth, lately I don't like the story.

CHAPTER
Mirror, Mirror
2

"So, what are we going to do about Conner's gig?" Tia asked Andy Marsden as he drove them to school on Monday morning.

"Conner's what?" Andy said, stopping at an intersection.

"His gig," Tia repeated. She glanced at Andy out of the corner of her eye as he checked his red curls in the rearview mirror. For a laid-back guy, Andy had quite a good relationship with reflective surfaces.

Andy turned to look her full in the face. "Conner has a gig?" A car horn honked behind them, and Andy slammed on the gas, flattening Tia against her seat.

"I knew it! I knew he wasn't going to tell you." Tia complained. "When was the last time you talked to him?"

"Yesterday," Andy answered, pulling into the Sweet Valley High parking lot. "What gig?"

"He's playing at House of Java," Tia told him as she removed a hair pick from her bag and fluffed her dark tresses.

"Are you serious? That's great!"

"Yeah, it might be great," Tia said, yanking violently at her hair. "If he had any interest in having an audience."

Andy maneuvered his huge vintage Cadillac into a space and reached over to grab the pick out of Tia's hand. "First of all, I don't think you want to be bald, so stop the abuse." He tossed the pick over his shoulder into the backseat. "Second, what are you so wigged about?"

Tia took a deep breath. "We're Conner's best friends, right?"

"I'm with you so far," Andy replied.

"So he didn't even tell me until yesterday, and he hasn't gotten around to telling you, and the show's this Friday," Tia said.

"As in four days from now?" Andy frowned. "What are we supposed to do? Just drop all plans?"

"That's the point! How does he expect anyone to show if they don't even know about it?" Tia popped open the car door and climbed out as Andy reached into the backseat for his backpack.

"I wonder how long *he's* known about it," Andy said, shouldering his backpack.

Tia raised an eyebrow. "Knowing Conner, probably for months." It was vintage McDermott. A teacher had once submitted one of his short stories to a county writing contest, and when it made the finals, Conner hadn't told a soul. Tia had only found out because she'd happened upon the letter when she was rummaging through his backpack for gum. As long as Tia had known him, Conner had dealt with bad and good news the same way—he didn't.

"So I've come to a decision," Tia said, pushing her thick hair behind her shoulders.

"Why do I have a feeling that this decision is not Conner sanctioned?" Andy asked as they wove their way between parked cars toward the school.

"Because you know us both so well," Tia answered. She crooked her arm around Andy's neck and pulled him close to her side, making it tough for both of them to walk.

"Well, I don't want any part of it," Andy said with a laugh. "I like to avoid the wrath of Conner at all costs."

Tia released him and shoved him gently. "What wrath of Conner? You're afraid of a shrug and an irritated sigh?"

"What can I say? I'm a wuss." Andy opened the school's front door for Tia, and she nodded her thanks as she passed through.

"I'm the one you should really be afraid of," Tia said, walking backward through the lobby to face Andy. "Or have you already forgotten how easily I used to pin you when we were little?"

"Good point," Andy said, stuffing his hands in his pockets. "What's the plan?"

Tia grinned. "Flyers," she said. "Angel and I are going to make up a load of them and pass them out everywhere. He's picking me up after practice, and we're hitting the copy shop."

"Oh, that's original," Andy quipped.

Tia ignored his comment. "Every student in this school is going to be so bombarded with Conner's face, they'll be afraid *not* to show." Tia leaned back against the locker next to Andy's.

"Conner is not going to like this," Andy said. "'Don't-notice-me' is his middle name. Did you know that? Conner Don't-notice-me McDermott—the Third." Andy laughed at his own joke.

"He'll be fine," Tia said. "He'll kick and scream, but he'll appreciate it in the end."

"Sounds kinky," Andy said. Tia slapped his arm. "I mean . . . uh . . . sounds like a lot of work."

Tia pulled his backpack from his shoulder and unzipped it for him as he popped open his locker. "That's why I've got friends like you." She held the backpack out to him, and Andy shoved his history book inside.

Andy groaned. "How did I know I was gonna be dragged into this?"

Tia smiled slyly. "Like I said, you just know me too well."

*   *   *

21

"Megan!" Elizabeth yelled at the top of her lungs as she adjusted the strap of her black tank top. "Have you seen my mascara?"

Conner walked into the bathroom and smirked. "I borrowed it. Sorry."

Elizabeth blushed. She would never get used to seeing Conner first thing in the morning. "Very funny." She was instantly hyper-aware of her disheveled hair and the tons of beauty products lying all over the counter.

"What?" Conner said. He reached around her back for a comb, his white T-shirt grazing her bare shoulder. Chills. "It makes my eyes stand out. That's very important, you know."

Elizabeth laughed, barely able to believe his easy manner. "You're in a good mood today," she said.

"Yeah, well, don't tell anyone." He slipped from the bathroom and closed the door behind him. Moments later a loud Led Zeppelin song filled her ears. Elizabeth was still smiling from their conversation when Megan popped her head into the bathroom.

"Use mine," Megan said, tossing Elizabeth a tube of mascara. "We're late, by the way."

"Shocker," Elizabeth said. She started to apply mascara to her top lashes. Ever since she'd moved into the Sandborns' house, Elizabeth had noticed herself becoming more and more Jessica-ish—as if she was making up for her sister's absence. She slept late, actually cared about makeup, and couldn't seem to keep her mind off guys. Well, one guy.

Elizabeth glanced at Megan, who had plopped down on the closed toilet and was picking through Elizabeth's brand-new makeup supply.

"So, Conner met my family last night when he came to pick Maria up after work—did he tell you?" Elizabeth asked. Totally natural.

"Nope. Didn't see him."

"Yeah? You must have gone to bed pretty early. You weren't around when I got home."

Megan carefully opened a blush compact and brushed some onto the back of her hand. "I went to the movies." She studied the color. "Didn't get home till after eleven."

Elizabeth took the blush from Megan and applied some to her own cheeks. "And Conner wasn't back yet?" she asked nonchalantly. Megan pulled a brush through her long, strawberry blond hair. "No, he wasn't. I think he got in pretty late."

What had he and Maria been doing till "pretty late"? A major pang of jealousy gripped Elizabeth's insides, and she angrily grabbed a tube of lipstick. *Maria's your friend, remember?* she reminded herself. *And Conner might be nice to look at, but he means nothing to you.*

Conner's stereo was silenced mid–guitar

solo, and Conner opened the bathroom door. He'd changed into a green T-shirt that accentuated his beautiful eyes more than any eye makeup ever could. So maybe he didn't mean *nothing*.

"Just thought you'd like to know the bus just pulled away," Conner said.

"Great," Elizabeth and Megan said in unison.

"Want a ride?"

Elizabeth couldn't believe he was actually offering. He'd warned them enough times that his old Mustang wasn't a taxi.

"Nah," Megan said, leaning back. "I think I'll just skip today."

Conner rolled his eyes and grabbed her arm. "Come on."

Elizabeth picked up her bag, and she and Megan followed Conner downstairs. They detoured through the kitchen to grab a quick breakfast snack for in the car and saw Mrs. Sandborn sitting at the table, holding her head in one hand and a mug of coffee in the other. She was wearing a thick terry-cloth robe, and her hair was sticking out Medusa style.

"Bye, Mom!" Megan said brightly.

"Bye, Mrs. Sandborn," Elizabeth said a bit more quietly.

Mrs. Sandborn groaned. "Bye, kids."

"She needs more caffeine," Conner said to

Elizabeth as he grabbed an apple from the basket on the counter.

"Like an IV," Megan said with a laugh as Conner held open the door.

Megan jogged over to the Mustang, popped the front seat forward, and held it, so Elizabeth crawled into the back. She silently thanked Megan. The last time Conner had driven her to school, she'd made a total moron of herself. She figured the less interaction with him, the better.

"So how was your date last night?" Megan asked her brother before they'd even backed out of the driveway.

Elizabeth's senses went on alert, but she crossed her arms and stared out the window as if she hadn't heard the question.

"It was great. Maria and I went to the Riot and then took a walk on the beach," Conner answered. "She is very . . . cool." His tone was full of innuendo.

A walk on the beach? Elizabeth knew what that meant. Couples never *walked* on the beach. They found a spot, laid out a blanket, put their arms around each other. . . . Suddenly the reason for Conner's uncharacteristically sunny disposition was all too clear.

"So when are you breaking up with her?" Megan asked point-blank.

Elizabeth looked up, and she saw Conner

glance at her quickly in the rearview mirror.

"I just love putting him on the spot," Megan explained.

"What are you talking about?" Conner asked, somewhat angrily. "I just said she was cool."

"Yeah, but that doesn't mean anything." Megan's voice sounded amused. "When has that ever meant anything?"

"I'm not breaking up with her," Conner said, adjusting his hands on the steering wheel. He wiped one palm against his thigh, glanced in the side mirror, and then looked at Megan. "I can't believe you said that."

Elizabeth watched his reflection in the rearview mirror, even though she could only see his brow and part of his right eye. Her heart was hammering with questions—none of which she could possibly ask. She was still staring in the mirror when Conner looked up again.

Elizabeth almost flinched and looked away, but she didn't. And this time Conner held her gaze for a good few seconds. She couldn't remotely read his expression. Finally he focused on the road again.

"No, I won't be breaking up with Maria anytime soon."

Jessica awoke from a bizarre dream that involved her mother and brother being on the cheerleading squad and Lila playing quarterback against a team of orangutans. She'd been shaken awake by freaky dreams all night, but this time when she looked at the digital clock beside the bed, it was finally morning. Monday-morning classes would start in less than an hour, but it didn't matter. She'd already told her mother she wasn't going to school today.

Jessica rolled out of bed, walked over to the window, and snapped the blinds shut. This was not a morning for a cheerful, sun-streaked room.

Maybe she should add a little gray eye shadow under her eyes to reconvince her mom she was really sick. She checked herself in the dresser mirror and knew there was no handiwork necessary. Her cheeks were pale, and there were dark half-moons beneath her eyes.

"What did you expect?" Jessica mumbled.

She stared at herself in the mirror, knowing that the worst thing to do when she was miserable was to think about all the things making her miserable, but she couldn't help it. She remembered the events of the last two weeks in rapid-fire succession. Will's kisses. Tia's note telling her Will had a girlfriend. Blabbing in the courtyard about what a loser said girlfriend must be. The moment at the dance when she'd realized who Melissa was and that she'd heard Jessica talking about her. "Jessica Wakefield is a slut" written across the blackboard. Lila and Amy siding with Melissa at the Riot.

That was the part that really took a sledge-hammer to Jessica's heart. Her so-called friends sitting by while Melissa's sidekick Gina called her a slut in front of everyone.

"Hi, Mrs. Wakefield!"

Jessica tensed as she heard Lila's muffled voice just outside her bedroom door. "I'm so sorry Jessica isn't feeling well."

Jessica's stomach clenched. She recognized that tone—Lila's "society" voice—polite and charming. She always said exactly the right things whether she meant them or not. Jessica shook her head, looking at the floor. Lila was so fake. Why had Jessica never called her on it?

"I was just bringing her some juice," Jessica's mother said. "Why don't you come in and say good morning?"

Jessica jumped up and threw herself back into bed, burrowing under the covers as the doorknob turned. Lila was standing slightly behind her mother. Jessica was surprised she hadn't made up an excuse to flee.

"How are you feeling?" Lila asked, flashing a smile as she walked into the room. She'd obviously decided it would be easier to live with Jessica and her parents if everything seemed all right on the surface.

"Worse, now," Jessica said pointedly.

Lila's eyes narrowed. "Oh, Jess. You're going to miss the first cheerleading practice," Lila said, her voice dripping with sugar. "But don't worry. I'm sure Coach Laufeld will understand." Jessica broke out in a cold sweat, unable to reply. She knew what Lila was implying. Missing practice—especially the first one—would be a huge black mark against her. The captainship was on the line, and everyone knew Jessica and Melissa were the top contenders. Melissa was about to have the edge.

Lila turned and smiled sweetly at Mrs. Wakefield. "I don't want to be late for school," she said. "I'll make sure Jessica's teachers know she's . . . ill."

"Thank you, Lila," Mrs. Wakefield said as Lila swept from the room.

She placed a glass of orange juice on the table next to Jessica's bed, then sat down on the edge of the mattress.

"You really don't look well," Mrs. Wakefield said, her eyes full of concern. She reached out and brushed Jessica's hair behind her ear with her fingertips. The strands tickled Jessica's cheek as they were pulled back.

Jessica almost burst into tears at her mother's touch. She bit her lip instead.

"I'm okay," she said shakily.

"Do you think you can eat?" her mother asked, still brushing.

"I'm not very hungry," Jessica answered softly, glancing up at her mother. "The juice will be fine, I think."

"Okay, honey." Jessica felt her mom studying her face. For a moment she wished she were little again. When she was sick, her mother used to stay home and bring her saltines and read to her. It was completely dorky, but she'd give anything to hear her mother read right now in that soft, husky, lull-you-to-sleep voice.

"Jessica, is everything okay at school?" her mother asked. Leave it to Mom to cut to the chase.

Jessica flipped over onto her back and looked at the ceiling as tears welled up in her eyes. It would be so easy to spill the whole thing. Tell her mom some losers were spreading rumors about her and making her life a living hell. But it was too humiliating. How could she say the whole school thought she was a slut? Besides, if her mother knew Jessica wasn't really sick, she'd make her go to school. That was not going to happen.

"Yeah, everything's fine," Jessica managed to say. "I think I just need a little rest." As much as she loved her mom, Jessica needed to be alone right now.

Mrs. Wakefield leaned over and kissed her daughter's forehead. "I think that's a good idea, sweetie. If you need anything, just call me at work."

"Thanks." Jessica turned back onto her side as her mother left the room, closing the door softly behind her. A tear slipped quickly down her cheek and spread into a stain on the pillow. A few moments later she heard a car engine start in the driveway, and then the house was uncomfortably silent.

She glanced at the clock again. Homeroom would start soon. Melissa would probably notice her empty desk immediately and gloat over a job well done. This afternoon she'd take charge at cheerleading practice.

Jessica pulled the white comforter over her head, forming a soft cave. She had never missed a practice in her life. But what did it matter? She'd only made the squad by the skin of her teeth. Melissa had already turned everyone against her. Jessica was sure they'd be glad to practice without her. She couldn't even imagine spending time with those people—Melissa, Gina, Cherie, Amy, Lila.

Maybe she should do herself a favor and just drop off the team. It wasn't like anyone would care.

*   *   *

31

Elizabeth slipped into homeroom just as the late bell rang.

"Well done, Liz," Mr. Collins said with a smile.

Maria waved Elizabeth over, grinning broadly. Elizabeth knew what that smile was all about, and she wanted no part of it. But there wasn't much she could do. She clenched her jaw and tried to quell the envy.

"You wouldn't believe what I did last night," Maria whispered when Elizabeth sat down.

"Made out on the beach, right?" Elizabeth said.

Maria's face fell. "He told you?"

"You don't expect a guy like Conner to keep quiet about his conquests, do you?" Elizabeth practically winced at her own catty words.

"Conquest? Thanks a lot, Liz," Maria hissed.

Elizabeth reached over and grabbed Maria's hand. "I'm sorry. Really. I just had a bad morning." She swallowed hard and prepared to say the unsayable. "I want to hear all about it."

Maria looked skeptical. "Really?"

No. Never. Please don't believe me. "Really," she said.

"Okay, well, after he picked me up at the restaurant ..."

Elizabeth forced a smile as Maria's rapturous tale unfolded all over her faux wood desk. God, she didn't want to hear this. But what choice did she have? Maria was her best friend, and Elizabeth was glad Maria was happy. She just wished Maria could be happy with another guy.

"Class, please quiet down and listen to the announcements," Mr. Collins said.

"I'll tell you later," Maria whispered.

Elizabeth telegraphed a mental thank-you in Mr. Collins's direction. She turned and opened her notebook as if there was something urgent she needed to get done before history class. She picked up her pen and started to scribble, pressing hard into the paper.

Note to self: Do whatever it takes to get over Conner and do it now!

TIA RAMIREZ & ANGEL DESMOND

THINGS TO DO:

~~CALL CONNER AND FIND OUT IF THERE'S ANYTHING HE WANTS OR DOESN'T WANT ON THE FLYERS.~~ (ANGEL POINTS OUT THIS IS A BAD IDEA SINCE CONNER WON'T WANT FLYERS AT ALL.)

FIND A GOOD PICTURE OF CONNER, PREFERABLY WITH A GUITAR.

HIT CONNER'S MOM UP FOR MONEY FOR THE FLYERS, AS WE ARE TOTALLY BROKE. (ANGEL'S NOT, BUT HIS MONEY IS ALL TIED UP IN SAVINGS FOR COLLEGE.)

CHECK OUT COPIES AND SUCH
AND MARTA'S STATIONERY FOR
THE LOWEST PRICE.

MAKE SURE CONNER HAS
SOMETHING OTHER THAN A
RIPPED T-SHIRT TO WEAR. (NOTE:
ANGEL DOES NOT AGREE, AS HE
BELIEVES CONNER'S
DISHEVELEDNESS IS PART OF
HIS CHARM.)

*****DON'T TELL CONNER
ABOUT ANY OF THE ABOVE.

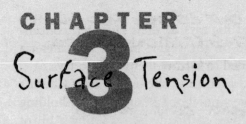
"I hear Jessica's out sick today," Cherie Reese said, tightening the ribbon holding back her long, curly red hair. She tasted her chef's salad and winced. "I guess that means she'll be missing practice."

Will Simmons crushed an empty soda can in one hand as Cherie brought up her friends' current topic of choice—the dissection of Jessica Wakefield.

"What a shame," Melissa said with a sigh.

"Yeah." Gina Cho crunched into an apple and spoke through a mouthful. "She's probably wiped out from entertaining the whole basketball team last night."

"You mean since the football team won't go near her anymore?" Matt Wells said. He let out his loud, obnoxious laugh and looked to Will for his approval. Will briefly considered punching Matt in his rather large mouth.

Melissa smiled. "Don't speak for the whole team, Matt," Melissa said. She looked at Cherie. "I hear the water boy may be interested."

Will closed his ears to their laughter, concentrating instead on the veggie burger the cafeteria staff had decided to torture them with today.

He studied Melissa as she leaned over Cherie's shoulder to see a notebook her friend was holding open. She seemed to finally be regaining a bit of confidence lately. What would she do if he defended Jessica?

"Personally, I think the squad would be better off without her," Gina said. "No one likes her. And I don't really think she should be representing the school. I can't believe she was actually captain last year."

Cherie flashed her a knowing look. "I bet she did more than stunting to get that position."

"You think?" Gina's eyes were wide.

"You are so naive." Cherie delicately wiped some bread crumbs from the front of her gold, V-necked T-shirt. "As a matter of fact, I heard she—"

Will couldn't take it anymore. "Did anybody get mustard?"

Melissa glanced at Will, her brow knitted.

"Rude much, Will?" Cherie asked. "I wasn't talking or anything."

"Sorry," he said. "But this burger is rank. I need something to hide the taste."

Melissa's expression softened, though not completely. She opened a packet of mustard and squeezed it onto his sandwich. "They are disgusting," she said, pushing hers aside. "Like dried-out rice and glue."

"Salad's not bad," Matt said, taking a huge bite. Will breathed a sigh of relief. Maybe Jessica bashing was done for the period.

"So anyway," Cherie said, leaning forward. "Lila was telling me about this guy Jessica used to—"

Turning his face toward a swirl of clouds outside the window, Will wished for rain. He'd love nothing better than to work out his frustration and guilt by shoving his teammates' faces into the mud at practice this afternoon. He cringed as Cherie let out her cackle of a laugh.

Changing the subject obviously wasn't going to work. But he had no other options. No matter how delicately he put it, no matter how subtly he hinted that Jessica wasn't who they all thought she was, Melissa would get upset. She was already insecure after what had happened between Will and Jessica. If he took Jessica's side, it would break Melissa's heart all over again. And Will couldn't handle the thought of causing her more pain. He still loved her.

The problem was, he cared about Jessica too. And Jessica hadn't even done anything wrong. He was the one who had cheated on Melissa. They should all be slamming him right now.

Melissa touched his shoulder. "Is everything okay? You seem kind of tense."

38

Will rotated his shoulders. He *was* tense. He forced a smile, a small stretch of his lips. "I can't handle this burger," he said. "I think I'll try the salad." He pushed back from the table and felt Melissa's eyes following him as he walked away. Hopefully, lunch would be over by the time he got back.

"Well, do you have a playlist yet?" Tia asked.

"Tee, can we talk about this later?" Conner responded. He had to grip the phone to keep the edge out of his voice. He wasn't even sure he had one song that didn't suck too much to play in public. "Don't you have practice or something?"

"Yeah, in about five minutes."

"You're calling me from *school*?" Conner demanded.

"What's your problem, Conner? We don't have much time to get ready for this," Tia complained. "Maybe if you'd told me about your gig earlier . . ."

Conner sighed.

"What are you going to wear?" Tia continued. "I think you should wear that blue velvet shirt I bought you last year."

Conner was so tense, his shoulders were practically kissing his earlobes. "The one that's rolled up in a ball at the bottom of Megan's closet?"

"Conner!"

"I gotta run," Conner stated.

"Fine," Tia said. "You deal with the music, I'll deal with the publicity. We'll work on your image later."

"Tia, leave my image out of this," Conner said. "And no publicity."

"But Conner—"

"I mean it, Tee," he said firmly.

"Okay, fine," she said, a bit too quickly.

"Swear?" Conner asked.

Tia huffed quietly. "I swear."

"All right. I'll talk to you later," Conner said. He dropped the phone back onto the cradle, sat down on his bed, and picked up his guitar. He knew Tia wasn't going to drop her promote-Conner campaign, but he figured it was a good idea to let his feelings on the subject be known. That way, if it all backfired, he could just blame her. Conner smirked. As if she'd ever take the blame for anything.

As he started to strum a few chords, Conner imagined walking off the stage and having some big-time agent hand him his card. He saw himself in a recording booth, complete with big headphones and a microphone hanging from the ceiling. Of course, there would also be a bunch of gorgeous groupies lounging in the plush dressing room, waiting for him to honor them with his presence.

"Yeah, right." Conner shook his head as he played. He already had more groupies than he could handle. And two of them were hanging out down the hall right now.

"Conner . . . Conner?" There was a loud rap on the door. "Conner!"

Conner stood up, crossed the room in one long stride, and flung open his door. Of course, Megan didn't really count as a groupie.

"What?" he shouted.

Megan jumped back slightly. "Bite my head off, why don't you."

Conner groaned. "I'm practicing."

"Sorry. Since when does practicing turn you into a psycho?" Megan asked. She glanced over his shoulder as if she thought there might be someone else in the room.

Conner reached out both arms and leaned them against the doorjamb to block her view. Let her wonder. He had some new lyrics lying out on the floor that he didn't want her to see anyway. "Since now."

"You're acting really weird," Megan said, narrowing her eyes. She crossed her arms over her chest. "Let me in."

Conner tightened his grip on the doorjamb. "No way."

"Whatever." She shrugged and turned to go. Just as Conner was relaxing his muscles, Megan turned around and dodged under his arm into his room.

"Megan!"

She stopped in the center of Conner's worn gray rug and looked around. "There's no one here."

"Sorry to disappoint," Conner said, shoving his hands in the back pockets of his jeans.

Megan turned around. She had a disturbing quizzical look about her. "So what were you hiding from me?"

Conner's eyes flicked to the floor, and Megan followed them. He lunged for his notes a moment too late. His little sister could be pretty fast when she wanted to be.

She picked up the papers and studied them. "'Stone Heart,'" she read aloud. "What's this?" She flipped through the papers, and recognition started to dawn in her eyes. "Are these lyrics? Are these lovey-dovey Conner McDermott lyrics?" She laughed, her green eyes dancing. "Are you auditioning to be the next Celine Dion?"

"You're very funny," Conner said drily. He snatched the papers from Megan's hands, then turned around to place them on his desk. At least she hadn't seen too much.

"Friday night. House of Java. Sound check, seven-thirty P.M."

Conner felt the tiny hairs on the back of his neck stand on end.

"Sound check for what, Mac?" Megan asked.

Conner looked at her. She was holding one last scrap of paper. Of course she'd managed to retain the one piece on which he'd written the info for his gig.

"Nothing," he said, knowing it wasn't going to work. He reached for the offending page. Megan held it out of his grasp.

"C'mon. I'm not that stupid. What's up?"

Conner glanced at the open door of his bedroom. "All right, I'll tell you. But you can't tell anyone."

Megan's eyebrows shot up. "My lips are sealed," she said, plopping down on his bed.

Conner walked over and quietly closed the door.

"Don't worry. Liz went over to her sister's after school," Megan said.

Conner glanced over his shoulder anyway. "Okay, the deal is, Gavin got me this gig at House of Java on Friday—"

"*This* Friday?" Megan interrupted, standing up.

Here we go, Conner thought. "Yeah, this Friday."

"Why didn't you tell me?" she squealed, grabbing his forearms. Conner had a sinking sense of déjà vu. "You're going to be playing in public!"

Conner wiped his hands on his jeans a few times, then shoved them under his arms. "Yeah."

43

"In front of hundreds of people!" Megan continued.

"I wouldn't say hundreds," Conner said.

"Can I at least tell Wendy and Shira?" Megan asked. "They'll kill me if they don't get to go."

Conner sighed.

"C'mon, Mac. They're my best friends!"

"All right," Conner said. "But just them." He knew it wouldn't mean anything, but he thought he'd say it anyway for the record. Now that Megan knew, HOJ would definitely be packed. "Thanks!" Megan practically skipped out of the room. "I'm so excited!"

"Yippee," Conner said under his breath.

He flopped back onto his bed a bit too fast and bashed his head into the headboard. He didn't even bother to rub away the throbbing. He was already defeated.

"So you've been *faking* the flu?" Elizabeth asked, pulling her feet up beneath her on Jessica's bed.

Jessica nodded and pushed her books aside to make room for both of them. "You don't know what it's like, Liz. They don't let up. And now Lila . . ." Jessica wrapped her arms around herself. "Let's just say I have no friends."

"Yes, you do," Elizabeth said.

"Name one," Jessica demanded.

44

"Um . . . hello?" Elizabeth waved her hand above her head.

"You don't count," Jessica said, picking at her nails. They were starting to chip, and she'd become obsessed with cracking the polish off herself. Funny. Lila had given her this manicure only last week.

"Thanks," Elizabeth said. She picked up the remote control and clicked off the television, which had been displaying a rather loud game show. "So what are you going to do, play sick for the rest of the year?"

"I wish," Jessica said morosely. "Do you think Mom would catch on?"

"There's a slim chance," Elizabeth said.

"Well, what am I supposed to do?" Jessica asked.

"First of all, stop hiding up here." Elizabeth pushed herself off the bed, walked over to the window, and yanked up the blinds. Jessica squinted in pain. "You're just making yourself more depressed."

Jessica held a pillow over her face to block the sunlight—and the image of Elizabeth's far too cheery face. A moment later Elizabeth pulled the pillow away and tossed it across the room. "And you look like death."

"That's helpful," Jessica said. She pushed her unwashed hair back from her face.

"I'm not kidding, Jess," Elizabeth said. "You're the one who always says to feel good you have to look good. Get off your butt and take a shower. You're polluting the room."

Jessica stood up and almost fell over. She'd barely moved all day, and her leg was asleep. "Are you trying to say I smell?"

Elizabeth looked her up and down. "You can move. That's a relief," she said.

"A shower is not going to keep everyone from talking about me," Jessica stated. "And it's not going to miraculously turn Lila into an un-bitch—"

"But not going to school is like admitting defeat!" Elizabeth said.

"You were the one who told me not to confront Will!" Jessica pointed out.

"Yeah, but I didn't mean you should drop out of life," Elizabeth said. "Besides, maybe hiding is like saying they're right. You have to . . . I don't know . . . fight back a little." Elizabeth perched on the edge of the bed and crossed her legs. Jessica looked down at her, wondering if her dear sister had finally lost it.

"What am I supposed to do? Attack the whole school?" She was practically shouting now, but the release felt good.

"Maybe," Elizabeth answered suggestively.

"And how am I supposed to do that?"

Elizabeth smiled. "I've been thinking about it," she said. "Isn't there a pep rally coming up?"

Jessica rubbed her temples. "Don't remind me. I've been seriously thinking about dropping off the team." Just saying it out loud brought Jessica close to tears.

Elizabeth's mouth fell open. "You're kidding."

"Do I look like I'm kidding?" Jessica managed to hold Elizabeth's gaze while her sister searched her eyes. When Elizabeth looked away, Jessica squeezed her eyes shut. She'd read somewhere that keeping them closed staved off tears more effectively than blinking.

"Jess." Elizabeth pulled Jessica down onto the bed by her wrists. "Quitting is the worst thing you can do. You'd just be handing Melissa your squad. I think the pep rally is exactly what you need."

Jessica's brow creased. "What have they been feeding you over at the Sandborns'?"

"I'm serious," Elizabeth said. "If you get up there and cheer in front of everyone like nothing's wrong—if you show them they're not affecting you—"

"Hold it right there, Liz." Jessica pushed away from her twin. "I appreciate the concern, but there's no way I'm going to subject myself to massive public ridicule. Going out there in front of all those people . . . it's like, 'Here I am! Abuse me!'"

47

"But that's the whole point! When people see you still have the guts to get out there—they'll ease up."

"You're really stretching, Liz." Nothing Jessica had done so far had stopped the torment. Certainly putting herself on display for the entire school like a big, fat bull's-eye wouldn't help.

"The only reason Melissa and her friends keep picking on you is because they know they *can*—don't you get it?"

Jessica shook her head doubtfully. It was easy for Elizabeth to make sense when the two of them were sitting in the relative safety of Jessica's bedroom. At the pep rally Jessica would be out on the floor by herself in front of the entire school. "I just don't think I can do it," she said.

"I know this sounds lame," Elizabeth said. "But you have to think positive. You have to get some of your confidence back."

"How?"

"Close your eyes."

"What are you going to do, hypnotize me?" Jessica glanced suspiciously at her twin.

Elizabeth laughed. "If I knew how to do that, don't you think I would have done it sooner? I mean, imagine all the arguments we could have avoided if I had just zombied you into doing whatever I told you to."

Jessica smiled. She shut her eyes. She was desperate enough to try whatever Elizabeth's plan was, even if it made her feel totally silly.

"Okay," Elizabeth said. "Now, I want you to imagine yourself on the basketball court doing your favorite routine. Got it?"

Jessica nodded.

"Okay. You're flawless out there, right?"

"Right." Jessica nodded, feeling beyond stupid.

"Good. Now, imagine Melissa and her friends are in the background picking on you."

Jessica shifted uncomfortably. One hand clutched the bedspread, and her eyes began to flutter open.

"No, no! Keep your eyes shut!"

Jessica forced her eyelids closed.

"Trust me," Elizabeth said. "Melissa and Gina and all those other losers are taunting you, but you're ignoring them. Going through your moves perfectly and ignoring them."

Jessica nodded. Okay. This was better.

"Coach calls your name, and you do some incredible tumbling run or whatever—"

Jessica grinned. Elizabeth's knowledge of cheerleading was so unimpressive.

"And then the whole school starts cheering and clapping for you."

Jessica savored the imaginary moment. "Maybe you're right," she said, slowly opening her eyes.

Elizabeth stood up. "Then you flash your devastating Wakefield grin." She smiled broadly. "And do that little Jessica saunter thing."

Jessica tried not to smile. "What Jessica saunter thing?"

"You know. Your little 'I'm not *trying* to wiggle my butt—that's just my natural walk' walk. Like this." Elizabeth started prancing around the room like an oversexed cartoon character.

Jessica flung a stuffed animal at her. "I do not walk like that."

Elizabeth dissolved into laughter. "I know. I'm just kidding."

Jessica stood up and hugged her sister. "Thanks, Liz," she said. For the first time in a long while she actually felt that everything might turn out all right.

Andy Marsden

Humorous Piece for <u>the</u> <u>Oracle</u>
<u>The</u> <u>Veggie</u> <u>Burger</u> <u>Solution</u>

The beginning of the school year's been tough on everybody—El Carro students forced to relocate, and Sweet Valley students forced to put up with it. Warring factions have popped up here and there, some schoolwide, some more personal. Even the gym hasn't been safe. Rumor has it a box of Ping-Pong balls is MIA, forcing Ping-Pong team trials to be postponed indefinitely, a disaster for any high school serious about sports.

Counselors and teachers have been at odds trying to figure out a way to solve the El Carro–Sweet Valley problem. But while they've been talking, the cafeteria food service has been taking action. Their solution: the veggie burger, a tasteless lump of matter on a bun.

Like all great ideas, the Veggie Burger Solution actually started out as an answer to a less pressing problem. Basically, to satisfy the adolescent appetite. The meal planners reasoned that as teenagers, grease and sugar are our nourishments of choice. Put a plate of delicately seasoned garden vegetables in front of us, and we turn as green as the broccoli. As far as we're concerned, vitamins are the province of fruit-flavored, candy-coated pills, preferably in the shape of our favorite cartoon characters. We won't touch anything that isn't either deep fried, dripping with melted cheese, or smashed into a round patty and wedged between a bun with the nutritional value of bleached cotton.

Charged with getting something wholesome into its students, the SOH head cook had an inspiration: Mince some vegetables to near death, mix them with leftover rice, add a little paste to hold it all together (preferably nontoxic), and form it into patties! The result—a stick-to-your-ribs feast fit for the garbage can, something every student at Sweet Valley High was able to agree on.

Thanks to the cafeteria staff, we have a reason to organize, to put aside our petty differences and fight for a higher purpose—the final obliteration of veggie burgers everywhere.

CHAPTER

The Benefits of Distraction 4

"I just hope she doesn't go after some other girl's boyfriend. I'd hate for anyone else to have to go through what I have," Melissa said, stretching her arms over her head at practice on Tuesday afternoon.

Lila smiled. "I know," she said. "But I wouldn't worry about it. The way Jessica's been looking lately, no guy will even glance in her direction."

"Yeah, did you see her today?" Cherie said. "I guess she was supposed to be sick yesterday, but she could have at least showered this morning."

Tia rolled her eyes. She was at the opposite end of the gym from the rest of the squad, and she could hear every word Melissa and her courtiers were saying. They were probably hoping Jessica would walk in and "overhear" their conversation. Pathetically obvious.

"Why don't they just leave her alone?" Tia asked Annie Whitman and Jade Wu—the only other girls on the squad who never participated in the picking apart of Jessica Wakefield.

Annie shook her head. "I don't get it," she said.

"Five days ago Lila was Jessica's best friend, and now—" She shrugged and slid her legs apart into a stretch. "I just don't get it."

"It's Melissa," Tia said, lifting her chin in the direction of the group.

"Yeah?" Jade was bent at the waist, and her head was touching her right knee. When she looked up, her long black ponytail fell over her face. "She seems so sweet most of the time."

"That's Melissa for you," Tia said. "Fragile as a butterfly until you piss her off."

"We'll keep that in mind," Annie said, straightening up.

Tia sat down on a mat and began to stretch her quads. She looked up at Annie and Jade, wondering what she could and couldn't ask. She was so bad at reading people. "Do you think Jessica did all the things they're saying she did?"

Annie's brow knitted, and she and Jade looked at each other. They glanced over their shoulders at the wolf pack in the corner, then settled down on the mat on either side of Tia. "Jessica's dated a lot, and it's not like competition ever stopped her from going after a guy," Annie whispered. "But she's not a slut."

"Why are you whispering?" Tia asked, leaning in close.

Annie looked over her shoulder again. Melissa and Cherie were studying them as they carried on their own conversation. "I don't want to get on their bad side, I guess," Annie whispered, blushing.

A loud squeaking of sneakers sounded from the gym door, and everyone looked up. Tia's stomach dropped as Jessica rushed into the room, flushed and flustered. She knew Jessica was in for it before Cherie even opened her mouth.

"Someone should tell her to save her extracurricular activities for *after* practice," Cherie said, her back to Jessica.

Tia pushed herself up off the floor. Jessica had frozen in the doorway, and Tia couldn't stomach the mortified look on the girl's face. Where was Coach Laufeld when they needed her? There had to be something . . . Then Tia remembered Conner's flyers.

"Hey, guys!" she called before turning to the bleachers. "I almost forgot. I have something for you."

She reached into her bag and pulled out the huge stack of fluorescent flyers she'd had printed at the copy shop. When she spun around again, she was pleased to see that she'd stolen the attention away from Jessica, who was quietly settling in by the wall.

"What are those?" Gina asked, her face creased with skeptical wariness.

"Flyers. Conner has a gig this Friday," Tia said, darting a glance at Jessica. She looked up with moderate interest, but reconcentrated her attention on her stretching when she saw Tia looking.

"Conner McDermott?" Cherie raised a perfectly plucked eyebrow. Tia knew the girl had been crushing on Conner since she was a zygote. Her outward calm couldn't mask it. Still, Cherie managed to cross the room at a slow, disinterested pace.

Melissa shrugged, and she and the others joined Annie, Jade, and Tia by the bleachers. Gina picked up one of the flyers and crinkled her nose. "I hate to say it, Tia, but isn't he a little green?"

Tia grinned. "They were supposed to be white with a fluorescent green *border*," she said. "But they gave me a ten-dollar price cut for the mistake."

"Conner the frog," Melissa said, studying a flyer.

"It's not easy being green," Gina added with a laugh.

Everyone else giggled, but Tia didn't care. The flyers would still do the job of advertising Conner's show, and Jessica was stretching out in peace.

"Just tell everyone he's the new Irish import star," Tia said, unloading a stack of flyers into Melissa's arms.

"What am I supposed to do with these?" Melissa demanded.

"Just pass them out in your classes, okay?"

Melissa made a face. "No, thank you."

"Girls? What's going on here?" Coach Laufeld had crept up on them out of nowhere.

"Hi, Coach!" Tia said cheerfully. "I'm kind of managing a friend's music career, and I was just asking everyone to help me pass out flyers."

Coach Laufeld picked up one of the papers and flicked her eyes over it. "McDermott," she said. "He's a student here, right?" She clipped the flyer to her clipboard.

"Yep," Tia said.

"Well, I hope all you girls will help," Coach Laufeld said to the squad. "Part of your job as spirit leaders should be to support all the students at this school when you can. Got it, Fox?"

Melissa blushed a deep crimson. "Right. That's just what I was saying." She grabbed another stack of flyers from Tia and placed them on top of her duffel bag. Tia grinned as the rest of the girls took small piles. With the cheerleading squad acting as his personal publicity group, Conner was sure to draw a crowd. Of course, he wouldn't be too happy if he knew of his association with the rah-rah girls, but she'd deal with that later.

Coach Laufeld told the squad to get into formation, and Tia was about to stuff the flyers back in her bag when she heard a voice at her shoulder.

"I'll take some."

Tia placed a few papers into an outstretched hand and followed the arm up to Jessica's face.

"Thanks," Tia said with a smile.

Jessica's lips twitched almost imperceptibly. "Thank you."

Elizabeth closed the door to her bedroom and locked it behind her even though she knew the house was deserted. The place was so still, it made her feel like she was on a stealth mission. Conner's music had become a constant background noise, and the house felt museum quiet without it.

"Good," Elizabeth said as she pulled a cardboard box from the shelf in her closet. "The less Conner, the better."

She lugged the box to her bed and dumped the contents onto the pristine white bedspread. Letters fluttered out as diaries and notebooks thudded onto the mattress and fell open in front of her. Elizabeth smiled. *So much for Conner,* she thought.

"It's time for a potent eye-opener." She greedily grabbed a blue envelope and removed the folded note.

Dear Liz,

It's too late to call, but I just couldn't fall asleep tonight without telling you how much I love you. You're my everything.

Love, Todd XOX

Elizabeth's heart warmed. This was such the perfect plan. Things might not have worked out between her and her ex-boyfriend, Todd, but they'd parted on good terms. And Elizabeth couldn't deny that he had always been sweet, romantic, and thoughtful. Three very un-Conner qualities. This trip down memory lane was exactly the wake-up call she needed. She grabbed another letter.

Dear Liz,

What's going on? You weren't home when I called after school and when I checked with Enid to see if you were there, she acted kind of suspicious, like something was going on. You're not seeing another guy, are you? I mean, after what happened between you and Joey Mason—you kissing him and everything—I can't help wondering sometimes if maybe you think of other guys besides me. This *is really bothering me. We need to talk.*

—Todd

Okay, so maybe Todd had insecure tendencies. But didn't everyone? There must be more *good* letters. She rummaged through the box, but simply found a bunch of notes passed in school—meet-me-at-Dairi-Burger, see-you-tonight kind of stuff. A lot of Xs and Os. Cute but not killer.

Well, Todd never was much of a writer. But Elizabeth was. It was time to hit the diaries. Conner would never measure up to her descriptions of Todd.

Wednesday, 1:15 P.M.

Dear Diary,

I don't know what to do. This guy in my math class asked me out, and if Todd finds out, he'll kill him. Should I tell him or hope he doesn't hear about it? I think Lila saw—

Elizabeth groaned. Had she really been that melodramatic? She leafed through the pages. A lot more of the same—looking at other guys, feeling guilty (her hormones had obviously been out of control last year), a few "popcorn and videos with Todd" entries. But there was none of the amazing, passionate feedback she'd been looking for.

She flipped forward a couple of months.

Friday, 12:17 A.M.

Dear Diary,

Todd won a stuffed animal for me at the carnival tonight. He spent ridiculous amounts of money on that stupid balloon-dart game until he won the biggest bear possible. He is so sweet.

Cute. But where was the passion? The all-consuming love? The heart-pounding intrigue? Elizabeth turned the page.

Monday, 3:15 P.M.

Dear Diary,

I am so stupid. Todd overheard me telling Enid that I thought Ken was cute and he freaked out. He's not talking to me anymore, and I'm afraid he's going to break up with me. I'm such a jerk!

"Ugh!" Elizabeth slammed the diary shut and tossed it across the room. "How immature can you be?"

Todd had stopped talking to her because she thought Ken Matthews was cute? She had felt guilty for thinking someone else was attractive?

"How totally lame," Elizabeth muttered, staring at the pile of memorabilia in front of her. This was not working out.

Elizabeth climbed off the bed and began to pace the room. When she reached her dresser, her eyes fell on a framed photograph of her and Maria at Crescent Beach from the Fourth of July picnic. Elizabeth picked it up and stared at Maria's smiling face. She and Maria had been best friends forever, and Elizabeth wasn't about to let a guy come between them. It was one of the standard feminist mantras—no man was worth ruining a friendship over.

"Especially not this one," Elizabeth said, replacing the frame. But what could she do? Not only was Conner living in her head, he was living in the same house. How could she ever get him off her mind when he was constantly assaulting her senses? His bedroom was just a few feet away.

Elizabeth spun around and looked at the door

62

as if she'd been startled. His bedroom. It was so obvious, she couldn't believe she hadn't thought of it before. Conner was a total slob—worse than Jessica, if that was humanly possible. She'd caught a glimpse of his room a few times when he'd left the door that connected to the bathroom open. Maybe comparing him to Todd wouldn't work, but at least looking at Conner's room should remind her of how totally wrong he was for her.

Elizabeth had never appreciated slacker slobs.

Nobody was around. If she was going to do this, she had to do it now. The perfect opportunity to put her plan into action.

After checking the hallway for any signs of life, Elizabeth tiptoed to Conner's room. She peeked inside, making doubly sure she wasn't about to walk in on Conner and totally humiliate herself. No one was there, so she pushed the door wide open.

"Oh . . . my . . . God." It was worse than she thought. What looked like a year's worth of clothes were thrown all over the place—socks hanging from lamps, T-shirts crumpled into grimy balls. It was enough to turn off even Jessica, the queen of sloth.

Elizabeth glanced to her left and winced. There was an encrusted cereal bowl on top of the dresser right next to her face. Two green Froot Loops were stuck to the rim. There was a pair of boxers lying next to it and . . . ugh . . . a half-eaten piece of pizza crust.

Elizabeth took a steadying breath. "That'll do it," she said, starting to back out of the room. She was sure that image would work as a libido crusher for weeks, if not months.

Then she saw his bookshelf. It was full of leather-bound classics. Elizabeth recalled Megan saying something about Conner saving painstakingly for the books when he was a kid. On top of the shelf, leaning against the wall and curling at the edges, was a picture of Conner when he was about twelve, looking with adoring eyes at a man she knew must be his father. She could see the resemblance even through the thin film of dust.

Elizabeth caught herself before her heart melted. So he had a couple of endearing qualities. Overall, he was a jerk. *And* a slob.

Elizabeth stooped and gingerly picked up a grungy black T-shirt between her index finger and thumb. "This ought to help," she muttered, eyeballing the worn-out piece of clothing. It was a ridiculous idea. She couldn't believe she was really going to do something so . . . gross, but Elizabeth was getting desperate.

She quickly pressed the disgusting garment to her nose and inhaled deeply, expecting a rank odor.

Instead, the musky warmth of aftershave

mixed with clean male sweat filled her nostrils. Elizabeth flashed back to a moment alone with Conner in his car. A moment when she'd wanted to grab him so badly, she'd had to bite her tongue to keep from doing it. Without thinking, she took another breath, forgetting where she was, lost in Conner's essence. Her eyes drifted closed as she imagined him there, holding her in his warm arms. She saw his piercing green eyes, could practically feel his kiss, their breaths mingling.

"Conner," she murmured.

Suddenly a door slammed and Elizabeth jumped, snatched from her fantasy. Her eyelids popped open, and she looked in horror at the dirty T-shirt crumpled in her hand.

She tossed the shirt to the floor, checked it, readjusted it into a ball, then ran from the room. Elizabeth had never felt so totally disgusted with herself.

Conner walked into the Riot on Tuesday night and barely had time to adjust his eyes to the darkness before a pair of slim arms encircled his neck.

"There you are!" Maria cooed, like they were a couple who'd been kept apart too long. Conner eased her arms off him. He was here to relax, and he didn't want anyone invading his personal space.

"Hey," he said, looking at the dance floor, the bar, the ceiling. Everywhere but at Maria's puppy eyes.

"So, what's new?" Maria asked, latching onto his arm.

"We only talked two hours ago." He started to weave through the tall pub tables near the door, making it impossible for Maria to hold on to him.

"Well, what's new in the last two hours, then?" Maria yelled to be heard over the music. Her tone was a little too cheery. She'd obviously caught the irritation in his voice.

Conner decided to ignore the question. "Come on," he shouted, not bothering to look at her over his shoulder. "I need a drink." He led her to the bar nestled beneath a second-floor overhang. The Riot sold only nonalcoholic beverages, which meant a near beer would have to do. Conner checked around for some of his more party-ready friends. Maybe one of them had smuggled in something with a little more kick. But as far as he could tell, none of the guys were there yet.

Conner bought himself a beer and Maria a Coke—her sole beverage of choice. She sipped her soda and moved her shoulders slightly, unconsciously, to the music. Maria really was beautiful, and she had moves on the dance floor that were probably outlawed in forty-eight states. But Conner wasn't in the mood to dance.

"Let's go upstairs," he said, reaching for her hand. The third floor was a sort of lovers' retreat—wine-colored couches and cozy chairs, romantic tunes pouring out of several strategically placed speakers. He and Maria had spent most of their time together up there, nestled in a particularly dark corner.

For the first time since he'd known her, a cloud of irritation passed through her eyes. "I'd rather hang out down here for a while," she said.

So she was actually capable of disagreeing with him. This was an intriguing development. Conner didn't even realize he was staring at her in muted surprise until she started backpedaling.

"I mean, we *can* go upstairs if you really want to, but I sort of feel like dancing—"

"Hey, you two!"

Conner had never been happier to hear Tia's voice. He wasn't quite sure how to take Maria's sudden flash of backbone followed by said backbone's complete disintegration. He liked the backbone.

"What's up, Tee?" he asked, planting a quick kiss on her cheek.

Tia grabbed Maria's wrist. "Come sit with us. Andy and I need some new blood to keep ourselves from looking like an old married couple." Maria slid off her stool and followed Tia. Conner brought up the rear.

"Where's Angel?" Conner called, sidestepping a giggling trail of bathroom-bound girls.

"He had to work late," Tia said, reclaiming her seat next to Andy.

"Is Elizabeth here?" Maria asked. Conner looked away and took a swig of his drink.

Out of the corner of his eye he saw Tia shake her head as she crunched on some ice. "She said she had too much work to do, but I don't know. I think she might be on a date." Tia grinned like a girl in the know.

"What makes you say that?" Maria asked, leaning forward.

"Just the distracted way she turned me down," Tia said. "Like, 'I can't. I mean . . . I have to work and I . . . I promised my sister I . . .'" Tia pretended to hold up a phone as she mimicked Elizabeth. "Totally covering something."

"Hmmm . . . maybe she's back with Todd Wilkins?" Andy suggested.

"Who's Todd Wilkins?" Conner instantly hoped those words had come from anyone's mouth but his own. Unfortunately, everyone was looking at him.

"He's Elizabeth's ex-boyfriend," Tia informed him. "She pointed him out to Andy and me the other day. Major, *major* hottie. Total superjock. Apparently they were together since birth."

"I don't think she's back with him," Maria said.

She shimmied out of her jacket and hung it on the back of her chair. Conner glanced at her skin-baring tank top, but couldn't appreciate it.

"Why?" Tia asked.

"Well, for one, she would have told me," Maria said. She took a sip of her soda and placed the glass on the table. "Second, he's right over there, undoubtedly engaged in a heated debate over next week's football strategy." Maria pointed across the room to a bunch of generic jocks, all wearing their varsity jackets.

Lame. But which one was Elizabeth's boy wonder? Elizabeth must have already pointed him out to Tia and Andy, because no one asked Maria which one he was. Conner wasn't about to show any more interest than he already had.

"So, the mystery continues," Tia said suggestively. Conner tuned his friends out as they engaged in a debate over Elizabeth's possible new love.

Maria wrapped both her arms around Conner's biceps and rested her head on his shoulder. He looked down at her upturned face—those melting eyes—and let his gaze travel over her bare shoulders. She was very sexy. He just really wasn't in the mood to appreciate it anymore.

"Still want to go upstairs?" Maria whispered.

Conner shook his head. "Not now."

Maria sat up straight, her eyes wide. "What did I do?"

"Nothing, all right?" Conner snapped. Maria leaned back stiffly in her chair and stared at the table. Conner saw her eyes well up and regretted his outburst. He didn't want to hurt her feelings, and he definitely didn't want to put a depressed spin on the evening. He just wished people could take no and yes for answers and not always prod for a deeper explanation.

Conner gulped down the rest of his drink and looked up at Tia. She was giving him the glare of death. Conner wasn't surprised—he was due for his hourly dose of guilt from someone.

A slow tune came over the speakers. "Hey, I love this song!" Tia said. "Come on, Andy." She grabbed Andy's arm and dragged him off his chair. "Why don't you guys join us?" Tia asked Conner pointedly. Andy shrugged at Conner and followed Tia to the dance floor.

"Wanna dance?" Conner asked.

Maria toyed with her soda glass. "Not until you tell me what I did," she said.

Conner turned to face Maria. "Look, I'm sorry I bit your head off," he said. "All I wanted was to have some fun tonight."

Maria looked up at him. Part of him hoped she would tell him to shove it and walk out herself— show the backbone again. But then she smiled, and he knew that wasn't going to happen.

"Okay, let's have some fun," she said meekly.

Conner took her hand and led her to the dance floor. At least he'd passed through the pouty part of the evening without any visible scars.

He wrapped his arms around Maria's waist and held her close. They fell into the standard, turn-in-a-slow-circle-while-swaying dance. Conner was just starting to get into the moment when their little turn motion forced him to face the jock pack again. Will Simmons laughed and clapped a tall guy on the back.

"Wilkins, you are the man," Will said. Conner's eyes narrowed as he watched the thumbheads.

"What're you thinkin'?" Maria asked quietly.

Conner pulled Maria to him and pressed his lips against hers. He felt her go limp in his arms. The pouty part of the evening was over for both of them.

Melissa Fox

It happened again. Tonight, when Will and I were out with some of our friends and the subject turned to Jessica Wakefield, he got up and went to the bathroom. Why is he doing that? No one likes Jessica. Everyone hates her for what she did to me. They stick up for me because they're my friends. And Will should be sticking up for me more than anyone. He's the one Jessica went after. He knows better than anyone how she is. But I've been noticing lately that whenever anyone starts talking about her, Will gets quiet or changes the subject.

He doesn't think I know. He thinks he's being ultra-subtle. But I can read Will's moods, and when people talk about her, it makes him extremely uncomfortable. That bothers me. A lot.

CHAPTER
Never Look Back
5

"And finally, the captain of our varsity cheerleading squad, Jessica Wakefield!" Coach Laufeld called out over the microphone. Cheers and whistles erupted from the crowd. Jessica heard a voice yell out, "Go, Jess!" Elizabeth could be heard over everyone.

Jessica paused the videotape from last year's pep rally and stared at her smiling, happy self frozen in time. It was Tuesday night, and she was home alone. Her parents had gone out to dinner with friends. Lila was out—probably hanging with Melissa, and here she was—watching a tape from long ago, trying to psych herself up. It wasn't *too* hard. She had actually been a pretty decent cheerleader.

"Who am I kidding? I dominated," Jessica whispered.

Starting up the tape again, she watched herself with an amazed longing—she'd been so carefree and happy then.

But all that had changed. The earthquake had

taken away part of it—seeing people hurt and lives destroyed wasn't something you could forget. But senior year was supposed to help her get over the quake—parties, checking out the coolest colleges to apply to, walking the halls and having all the underclassmen scurry to get out of her way.

Now even freshmen were laughing behind her back.

Jessica felt herself falling into a depression again and tried to talk herself out of it.

"It's not like the year's over," she said aloud. "And after the pep rally, Melissa will just fade into the background."

Jessica watched as the squad performed the dance routine. She picked out the missteps, the few uncoordinated arms. She remembered working with the squad every day—hammering out every last detail so she could take them to the championships. Jessica's eyes flicked to her second-place trophy from the nationals. No one could take that victory away from her. Least off all a hack from El Carro. Jessica got up and walked over to the shelf to dust off the trophy.

Suddenly the cheering stopped, and Jessica heard Lila's voice coming from the television speakers. "Oh, Jess, you are just the *goddess* of cheerleading! We all want to be *just like you!*"

Jessica heard her own laugh and turned around to face the screen. The squad was gathered in the lobby, messing around after the pep rally. Lila was down on one knee, kowtowing to Jessica in mock worship.

"Oh, please, Lila," Jessica said, fanning herself primly. "I just can't take all the flattery." Lila laughed, and Jessica pulled her up from the floor.

Jessica told herself to shut it off, but she just stood there, frozen, watching herself throw her arm around Lila and wave at the camera. Amy Sutton ran by and flung up their skirts, then took off with Lila chasing her. Jessica felt sick to her stomach. They didn't even talk to her now. How was she ever going to keep up her confidence with all of their negativity surrounding her on the court?

Jessica sat down on the bed, reached for the phone, and started to punch in Elizabeth's number. But she hung up before she finished. Elizabeth was probably out with her friends. She actually had a few.

"Hey, Jess," a deep voice called from off camera. Jessica saw Ken Matthews saunter onto the screen. He picked her up and twirled her around. "You were awesome." He lowered her and planted a kiss on her nose. Jessica had to choke back a sob. There they were—Sweet Valley High's star quarterback and the captain of the cheerleading squad. Destined for the "class couple" category in the back of the yearbook. But that was before Olivia.

Before the earthquake. Before Melissa. Now Ken was a total loner and Jessica was an outcast.

Jessica finally turned off the VCR. She had to talk to someone. She grabbed the phone again. If Elizabeth wasn't there, at least she could hear her sister's taped voice and leave a message.

Jessica punched in the numbers and waited for the phone to ring—once, twice, three times—and then Elizabeth answered.

"I'm so glad you're there!" Jessica flinched, hearing the desperation in her own voice.

"Is everything all right?" Elizabeth asked anxiously.

"Yeah, I'm okay," Jessica said, infusing her voice with calm.

"Good. So what's up?" Elizabeth asked.

"Nothing, really," Jessica said. "Do you wanna come over? I was just watching some old videotapes, and—"

"Oh, Jess, I'm sorry. I can't tonight." Elizabeth sounded a little harried. "I'm right in the middle of editing this rush article for the *Oracle* and I'm sort of on a roll."

Jessica's heart fell. Dissed for the *Oracle*? How low could she go?

"Why don't we have lunch tomorrow?" Elizabeth asked. "We could go off campus."

"Tomorrow?" Jessica echoed. She needed to talk to someone now. Just knowing she wasn't alone would make her feel so much better. But a little voice inside her head told her to take what she could get. She didn't want to get all whiny and risk alienating Elizabeth too.

As soon as Jessica had that thought, she realized how sick it was. Elizabeth would never turn her back on her. Even if all the things being said about Jessica were *true*. But it was really hard to fight the rejection reflex at this point.

"Jess?" Elizabeth was waiting for an answer.

Jessica swallowed her disappointment. "Sure," she said. "Tomorrow's great."

"Good. I'll see you then."

Jessica held the receiver for a moment, listening to the disconnected line. Then she sighed, picked up the remote, and clicked off the TV. There was no reason to watch anymore. Jessica felt pathetic enough already.

"Conner, wait. Stop."

Conner pulled away from Maria and rolled onto his back. "What's the matter?"

Maria sat up, adjusted her shirt, and pushed her hands through her short hair. "I'm just . . . I don't know. Everybody's here."

Conner glanced at the bonfire down the beach and sighed in exasperation. Andy, Tia, and some of the guys Conner occasionally hung with were milling around. A few other couples made shadows along the outskirts of the fire. That's what Crescent Beach was for. Partying or making out.

"They're not paying any attention," Conner said, leaning on one elbow. He reached up with his other hand and ran a finger down Maria's cheek. "Besides, who cares what they think?"

"I do," Maria said. "I also care what I think."

Here we go, Conner thought. "And what do you think?" he asked, sitting up fully. He stared out at the ocean, ethereally blue in the moonlight.

"I think I want to know what *you* think before I—before we—" She giggled nervously and looked down at the sand. "You know."

"What I think about what?" Conner asked. He picked up a pebble and flung it toward the water. This was so frustrating. He knew exactly what Maria was talking about. He'd heard it from other girls, and he'd hoped he and Maria could have some more fun together before they got around to this conversation.

"About us," she said, looking up at him. "What do you think about us?"

Conner looked into her dark brown eyes and, for a moment, wished he could tell her what she wanted to hear. That he wanted a relationship. That he wanted only her and wanted to be with her at every possible moment. Only none of it was true.

"I think I'm gonna go get something to drink." He stood.

Maria scrambled to her feet. "Conner—"

"What?" He shoved his hands into the back pockets of his jeans and hoped she wouldn't make him say it. For once, he didn't want to see the backbone.

"Nothing," Maria said. "Forget it." She walked around him and headed for the bonfire. Conner stood and watched her go, knowing she wanted him to follow, apologize, and profess his undying love.

Conner turned and cut through the reeds, heading for the parking lot. He'd had enough "relaxation" for one night.

Elizabeth stared at the phone, wishing she had told Jessica the real reason she was home. Tia and Andy had asked her to go to the Riot, but she knew Maria and Conner were going to be there, so she had sequestered herself for the evening.

Elizabeth had tried to get her work for the *Oracle* done, but her mind kept wandering to ways to get over her obsession with Conner. She could never have explained *that* to Jessica without sounding like a total loser. She would make up for it tomorrow at lunch. Tonight, she was going to put aside the *Oracle* and get some nonschool reading done.

Elizabeth had bought the new issue of *Mademoiselle* that afternoon. After her other little plans had failed, she had decided to get out of the house. She'd hit the bookstore, a place that always seemed to calm her nerves. As she was wandering among the shelves, she'd discovered that one of her favorite authors had just come out with a new book. Elizabeth decided to splurge, and when she was waiting on line, a headline on the magazine had caught her eye.

"America's 10 Most Influential Women." A fashion magazine doing an article on female power players? This she had to see.

But when she'd returned home and cracked open the magazine, another article had jumped out at her. "Are You Obsessed? Take This Month's Quiz and Find Out!" At first Elizabeth thought the idea that a silly quiz could help with a real problem was just that—silly. But the article was actually written by a psychologist. And when she skimmed the questions, they seemed pretty legit. Elizabeth wasn't into New Age thinking, but it did seem as though fate had put the magazine in her way.

Shoving her pillow against the headboard of her bed, Elizabeth opened the issue to the quiz. She read the title—"Is It Love or Obsession?" Obviously it wasn't love. But just how obsessed was she?

She scanned a list of true-or-false questions.

You can't stop thinking about him, even though there's no real relationship between the two of you.

Elizabeth cleared her throat. Okay, so that was sort of true. Although she did technically live with

Conner, which might constitute a relationship. But she decided to be honest. She grabbed a pencil from her bedside table and circle the *T*. After all, no one was going to see her answers, and the whole point was to get over Conner, not to come out smelling like a psychologically perfect rose.

You want to stop thinking about him, but find it impossible.

Elizabeth reread the question. She bit her lip, her pencil poised over the *F*. This was stupid. Of *course* she wanted to stop thinking about him—why else would she be taking this quiz? She circled *T*.

You believe your life is meaningless without him in it.

Elizabeth heaved a relieved sigh.
"Finally." She circled *F*. She wasn't *that* low on the self-esteem chain.

He spurns every advance you make.

Elizabeth flipped the page to the end of the quiz. There was a little picture of the author, along with a minibiography. "Dr. Jeffrey P. Green," she read aloud. "Well, Jeff, you sure know how to make a person squirm."

She flipped the page back and read the question again. If she'd actually made any *real* advances toward Conner instead of just turning into a total spaz around him, she figured he would either laugh in her face or spontaneously vomit. Conner obviously wasn't interested in her other than to make her feel like an idiot whenever possible. That was a *T.*

You consider your feelings to be a problem.

"Rub it in, why don't you?" She circled *T.*

Elizabeth slumped against the headboard. Great. She was an obsessed freak. But she was not going to beat herself up about it. *Cut the crap, Wakefield,* she demanded. *It's time to get over this jerk.*

Elizabeth decided to forgo the multiple-choice questions and checked the obligatory advice column that followed. "What to Do If You Have Determined You Have an Obsession." She skipped the psychobabble opening paragraph and went straight to the suggestions.

(1) Humanize the object of your desire. Uncover his foibles and recognize that he isn't perfect.

Right. Well, she'd tried that already, and it didn't work. Elizabeth munched on her pencil. Dr. Jeff had probably spent hundreds of thousands of dollars on school. Couldn't he tell her something she hadn't already come up with on her own?

(2) Find other interests. Friends, hobbies, work, travel will all help you keep your mind off him/her.

"That would be fine if all my friends didn't worship the ground he walks on," Elizabeth muttered.

(3) Repeat to yourself that you are worthwhile, that you deserve someone who wants you as much as you want him/her.

Elizabeth closed the magazine. Okay, basically she was supposed to keep reminding herself that Conner was a jerk and she wasn't. She could do that. And she could concentrate on work—maybe take on a new club or something to keep her out of the house. Plus Conner had to have some reprehensible qualities other than being a slob. She just had to figure out what they were.

Feeling better, Elizabeth decided to get herself a snack. All this self-exploration had left her famished. She carried the magazine to the kitchen, figuring she'd read some of the middle parts while she ate.

She pulled some salsa and tortilla chips out of the cupboard, popped open a bottle of iced tea, and settled in at the kitchen table. Elizabeth flipped open to the advice column again.

Love is mutual. Often, a person will mistake sexual attraction for love. A person who is in love with you will show it in numerous ways. But sometimes when a man sees a woman is taken with him, he'll use that knowledge to get what he wants from her.

The back door swung open, and Elizabeth jumped. Conner walked into the kitchen.

Flustered, Elizabeth slapped the magazine closed, turned it over, and threw her arms over the back cover.

Conner eyed her suspiciously. "I thought you had a date."

Elizabeth blushed. "A date? Who told you that?"

"Forget it," Conner said, leaning on the back of the chair directly across the table from her. "What are you doing?" he asked. "You look like you just got caught cheating on your SATs."

Elizabeth nervously brushed some crumbs from the table. "Nothing," she said. "You scared me, that's all."

"You scare too easily." Conner glanced at the magazine Elizabeth was trying to hide as he walked to the fridge.

As he passed, Elizabeth caught a whiff of the same masculine sweat-aftershave aroma she'd inhaled in his bedroom.

He's a jerk, Elizabeth reminded herself. *You could do so much better.*

She looked away as he leaned over to check out the contents of the fridge.

He's not your type. Just look at his dirty, beat-up jeans. Elizabeth's eyes fell on the tear just above his knee as he turned around. *Or don't look at his jeans,* she thought, blushing.

He's dating your best friend. He's conceited. He's rude. She studied her iced-tea label as she listened to him gulp down a soda, then toss the can into the recycling bin.

"Well," Conner said. Elizabeth finally looked at him. He was leaning back against the counter. There was a question in his perfect green eyes, but he didn't ask it. "Good night," he said in a low, gravelly voice.

It sent chills down Elizabeth's back.

"Night," Elizabeth responded.

He half-smiled, then turned to go. She heard

the stairs creak under his weight as he rushed upstairs.

Elizabeth was smiling. Just the sound of his voice made her melt. She let out a little groan of despair and dropped her head. Maybe she should read that advice column one more time.

Maria Slater

What people don't understand about actors is that it's often harder for us to hide our feelings than it is for almost everyone else. We can lend our emotions to characters, but it's not that easy for us to cover our true feelings in real life. Think about it. We're constantly reaching deep down into ourselves to access our emotions, so they're always right there on the edge. When I'm being me, I'm being me for real.

Conner's a deep person. He hides it, but I sense these amazing feelings beneath the surface that he's scared to show. The other day I came right out and asked Tia what Conner was so afraid of. Tia got annoyed (no problem showing emotions there). "If Conner's afraid of anything, that's Conner's business," she told me with the kind of loyalty I can only hope my friends feel for me.

So why do I insist on pushing Conner? I

know I've been acting clingy around him, and he hates it. I've even tried to make a character sketch for myself a sophisticated, slightly callous femme fatale. But once I'm with him, it all goes out the window. Because I'm not that. I'm not even remotely that. And the real me won't allow those fake feelings to rule. I'm who I am. And I think . . . God, I think I'm in love with him. And I want Conner to know the real me.

CHAPTER 6

A TURN TOWARD THE UGLY

Jessica forced herself to keep her chin up as she navigated the hall on her way to Ms. Dalton's eighth-period French class on Wednesday afternoon. Elizabeth had given her an award-worthy pep talk at lunch, and Jessica had spent most of the day trying desperately to follow her sister's advice. Chin up. Shoulders back. Eyes straight ahead and filled with purpose—as if there was somewhere she just *had* to be.

While she was talking with Elizabeth over pizza at Guido's, acting confident had seemed so doable. But walking down the school corridors alone, Jessica felt every giggle, every whisper, was aimed at her.

She passed a group of junior girls near the water fountain. No sooner had she walked by them than they broke into laughter. Jessica flinched. Were they laughing at her? *Stop it,* she ordered herself. *They're probably talking about something totally unrelated.* Still, the urge to hide—to keep her head down so she wouldn't meet anyone's eyes—was so strong.

She finally reached her classroom. As she stepped inside, she immediately met her sister's eye from across the room. Elizabeth smiled, and it gave Jessica the strength to reach her desk without looking at anyone else.

Jessica was about to sit down when she heard Cherie and Melissa's unmistakable giggles. On her chair was a cheesy photo of a naked woman from a men's magazine. The caption read, "I never met a man I didn't like." The model's head had been replaced with a photo of Jessica's taken from last year's yearbook.

Jessica's face burned as she crumpled the magazine page and shoved it into her backpack, too humiliated to get up and walk to the garbage pail beside the teacher's desk.

"I guess she's taking it home to add to her scrapbook," Josh Radinsky said loudly.

This was new. Jessica was usually left alone in French class. She had always assumed it was because Elizabeth was there. Now even eighth period wasn't safe.

Peripherally, Jessica saw Elizabeth start to get up from her desk, but then the bell rang and Ms. Dalton breezed into the room.

"Settle down, everyone!" she said over the classroom din. Jessica had to fight not to run from the room in tears.

She glanced at the clock above the front

blackboard. She just had to make it through the next forty-five minutes and then—her stomach flopped. And then cheerleading practice.

Cheerleading had become a horror show. If it wasn't for Annie, Tia, and Jade, practice would be pure misery instead of just an agonizing chore.

"Class, I want you to break up into groups of three and practice last night's dialogue," Ms. Dalton said. "You can go ahead and choose your own partners."

Elizabeth and Maria were by Jessica's side in a flash.

"What happened?" Elizabeth asked, taking the empty desk behind Jessica.

"I don't want to talk about it," Jessica said, her voice barely audible. She turned her desk to face Elizabeth's, grateful to have her back to the rest of the room she wouldn't have to see their taunting faces.

Maria gave her a sympathetic look as she settled in with her textbook next to Elizabeth. "It's not everyone, Jess," she said. "You know that, right?"

"Let's just do the assignment." Jessica opened her book.

Maria glanced worriedly at Elizabeth, then smiled a little too brightly at Jessica. "Jessica Wakefield did her homework?" she teased.

92

"It's not like I have anything else to do lately," Jessica said, flipping open her notebook.

Maria seemed unfazed. "You know what you should do, Jess? You should come with us to see Conner play at House of Java."

Jessica saw Elizabeth's brow tense almost imperceptibly.

"I saw the flyers," Jessica said. "I told Tia I'd give a few out, so I put them on the counter at Healthy." Jessica wasn't actually planning on going. She figured it was going to be a huge El Carro scene. But at least they were onto another subject. "Is Conner any good?"

Maria raised an eyebrow. "I've never heard him play, but he's good at everything else," she said, blushing deeply.

Elizabeth smiled, but she looked pained. Maria didn't seem to notice, but Jessica could tell something was bothering her twin. "You live with him, Liz," Jessica said, hoping to get her sister to spill. "Have you heard him practice?"

"Not really," Elizabeth answered, shifting in her seat. She was lying. "So, when's the big pep rally?" she asked. Then she straightened up in her chair. *"Excusez moi, s'il vous plaît. Est-ce que vous savez où est le téléphone?"* Jessica knew that meant Dalton was giving them the eye, so she read the answer.

"All right, she looked away," Maria said, leaning forward.

Elizabeth adjusted the shoulders of the low-cut, blue silk blouse Jessica had given her—a style Elizabeth would never have worn before and Jessica would probably never wear again.

Jessica self-consciously touched the collar of her gray turtleneck. "The pep rally's this Saturday, but they're not sure what time yet."

"I can't believe you can handle being with those losers every day, Jess," Maria said. "That takes guts. If it were me, I'd probably have quit the squad by now."

"It's not like I haven't thought about it," Jessica said.

"But you're not thinking about it anymore, right?" Elizabeth asked.

"No way." Jessica tried to sound more confident than she felt. Every minute at school and practice was torture. She didn't know what she dreaded more, walking through the halls where the jeers were tossed in an open forum or watching her ex-friends whisper about her between drills.

Jessica felt Ms. Dalton walk up behind her. "Ladies, I don't hear you speaking French," she said pleasantly.

"*Je m'excuse*, Mademoiselle Dalton," Jessica said automatically.

"Miss Wakefield, your accent is improving," Ms. Dalton said, patting Jessica on the back. "Keep it up."

Jessica sank lower in her seat, wondering what comment her classmates could come up with to follow that little spotlight. "*Merci*," she muttered.

"See, Jess?" Elizabeth whispered as Ms. Dalton moved on to the next group. "It isn't *all* bad."

"Right," Jessica said. "I just have to remind myself of my budding translation career."

"Hey, Mac, you wanna come out for burgers with Liz and me?" Megan asked as she passed by Conner in front of his bedroom.

"Thanks, but I'm not hungry," Conner said.

Megan froze. "I know you didn't just turn down burgers," she said as she tied her long, red-blond hair into a knot on top of her head. She stuck a chopstick into the bun, and it miraculously stayed.

"How do you people do that?" Conner asked.

"Tricks of the female trade your pea-sized brain could never possibly understand," Megan said. "So you're really not coming?"

Elizabeth called to Megan from downstairs.

"One sec!" Megan yelled.

"Thanks anyway," Conner said, glaring at the top of the steps. "But I've got . . . stuff to do."

Megan looked into Conner's room, where his guitar was lying on his bed. "Oh, preparing for the big night?"

"Hey, remember our deal," Conner hissed. He glanced at the stairs again.

"News flash, Mac. Elizabeth works at House of Java. She's known about your gig all along," Megan said, patting Conner on the shoulder for consolation. "Besides, it's all Tia talks about. She even has Elizabeth's sister handing out flyers."

Conner tipped his head back in exasperation. He didn't know what he'd been thinking. He'd totally forgotten about Elizabeth's part-time job. Of course she was going to find out. But then, she hadn't mentioned anything to him—hadn't asked him to play anything for her or read his lyrics like Maria had been doing every five seconds.

"I'll see you later," he said to Megan. He walked into his room and shut the door before she could respond.

Once he was sure Megan and Elizabeth had gone, Conner unplugged the phone and started to practice. He'd finally come up with a list of songs, and he wanted to play them straight through to see how they flowed.

As soon as he started playing, he knew he'd hit his stride. The riffs were great—fluid and strong, with enough variation to keep even the toughest audience interested. He did a complete run-through of the set. It all came together perfectly.

Then he came to the final song—"Stone Heart." It was trouble, definitely trouble. Not the

96

music—the lyrics. Did he really want to play it when Elizabeth might be there?

He strummed the first chord and sang.

"You catch a glimpse of sun-streaked hair—" Conner stopped and ran a hand over his brow. Sun streaked. That line was bothering him. Should he change it? To what? And more important, what for? This was California. There were a lot of girls walking around with blond hair. People who didn't have a single blond hair in their genes had blond hair.

"Break time," Conner said. He stood up and headed downstairs.

He could use a cold beer. But he never kept alcohol in the house because he would have to play keep-away-from-Mom. She'd been laying low lately—keeping her drinking binges confined to her room instead of out in public. She did this after every embarrassing incident at the country club, when he had to physically drag her to the car and drive her home because she was so tanked. But he knew from past experience that it wouldn't last long. It's not like she had stopped drinking—just that she was doing it alone. Sooner or later she'd decide to go out on the town again.

He rubbed his temples, wondering when the next crisis would occur. Why angst over it? There was nothing he could do. He'd learned that at an early age.

Conner grabbed a soda from the fridge. On his way to the living room, he passed the phone and noticed the answering machine message light was flashing. Conner dialed into the system and entered the pass code for his voice-mail box. There were three messages for him. He hit play. "Hey, man, it's Andy. Just wondering if you wanted to get something to eat later. Gimme a call."

Conner deleted the message and listened to the next one. "Conner, it's Maria. We need to talk about last night. Give me a call as soon as you get this, all right?"

Conner closed his eyes, irritated. Like he really wanted to talk about last night. He played the third message.

"Conner, where *are* you?" Maria again. "We've got to talk. Please call me back."

Oh, man. What was it with her?

He picked up the phone. Maybe he'd just call her and tell her it was over. But phone breakups never worked. Girls always made a scene the next time they saw him. It was like they needed to see his face to make sure he was really serious.

After a couple of rings, Maria answered.

"Hello?"

"Hey. I got your messages."

"And?"

"You're right. We have to talk. How about meeting me at First and Ten at seven tonight?"

98

"Great," Maria said, obviously relieved.

Conner didn't allow himself to feel guilty. What had to be done had to be done.

I can do this, Jessica told herself when she entered the gym for practice after school. The butterflies in her stomach were going wild.

"Okay, it looks like we're all here," Coach Laufeld said as soon as she saw Jessica walk through the door. Jessica had waited until the others were out of the locker room before changing. She couldn't stand the thought of being ranked on or stared down. She could feel them watching her now. All the people who hated her most assembled in one place. If Coach Laufeld hadn't been there, Jessica could bet there would be a lot more going on than dirty looks.

Coach Laufeld blew her whistle. "Okay, quit the chatter," she ordered the team.

Everyone quieted down and turned their attention to the coach. "I've got your standard formation here," she said, glancing at her clipboard. "You'll use this for all nonstunt cheers and sidelines, and I don't want to hear any whining about who's in front and who's in back. I did it in height order."

Jessica held her breath as Coach Laufeld assembled everyone into lines. She was hoping she'd be in the back so she could keep an eye on everyone

99

instead of the other way around. Of course, Renee Talbot and Cherie were much taller than Jessica, so she ended up in the middle line—right between Melissa and Amy. Tia, Jade, and Annie, her only allies, got the front.

"Okay, everyone take note of where you are," Laufeld said. "Got it?" Everyone nodded. "Good, now have a seat."

Jessica dropped to the floor with the rest of the squad, keeping her eyes trained on Annie's ponytail.

"Look, ladies, we've got a pep rally coming up and need to get in as much practice as possible, so I want you to be honest with me here." Laufeld looked at Melissa. "Can anyone from El Carro tell me what stunts you performed last year?"

"All of them," Melissa said simply.

"That's a bold statement," Coach Laufeld said with a smirk. "Can anyone else give me a more . . . detailed answer?" Melissa turned beet red, and Jessica had to concentrate hard to keep from grinning.

Tia raised her hand.

"Ramirez," Coach said.

Tia listed the stunts and added that most of their good bases had ended up in Big Mesa when the El Carro students were split up.

"That's okay. We have plenty of bases here." Coach Laufeld looked the squad over. "We're going to need three double-base extensions for the hello cheer. Lila, Jade, Amy, and Jessica—why don't you demonstrate for the rest of the team?"

Jessica's heart tried to escape through her throat. The double-base extension required her to place her feet into Lila and Amy's hands. Then they lifted her, standing, above their heads. Jade was their spotter. It was a stunt they'd perfected for nationals, but the idea of trying it with them now made Jessica extremely uncomfortable.

Jessica saw Amy and Lila shoot each other a look before they slowly stood up.

"Come on, Wakefield. On the mat," Coach said.

Jessica stood. She was shaking. Melissa was staring as if willing Jessica to wither before her. Amy and Lila stood facing each other. Jessica walked over and got in position for the prep— placing one hand on Lila's right shoulder and one on Amy's left. "You're shaking, Jess," Lila said. "Pull it together, or you're going to fall."

"I know," Jessica said. She took a deep breath. They weren't going to drop her unless she did something wrong. Laufeld would notice if Amy buckled intentionally or if Lila moved. She gave the count.

"One, two!" She jumped into their hands, and in one swift motion she was standing in the sky— higher than the basketball nets. She locked her knees and threw her arms up into a V over her head. She'd forgotten the heady feeling she got from stunting.

"Okay, bring her down," Coach said. Jessica's heart skipped a beat. She envisioned the fall into Lila, Amy, and Jade's arms and panicked. Here they could really get away with dropping her.

Lila gave the count. "One, two!"

"Wait!" Jessica squealed. But it was too late. Her feet went out from under her, and she was falling. She kicked her legs out like she was supposed to, but she was a split second off.

Jade cradled her under her arms, but Amy and Lila's arms gave way as she came crashing down. Her butt hit hard on the mat.

"Jessica, are you okay?" Jade asked. Jessica felt nothing but the pain in her tailbone. It had been a long while since she'd been dropped.

"Annie, go get some ice from the trainer," Coach Laufeld ordered, helping Jessica up. "That was sloppy, girls," she said, leveling Lila and Amy with a stare.

"What?" Lila squeaked. "She went limp!"

"I wasn't blaming anyone," Coach said, her hand on the small of Jessica's back. "This is a team. You're not to blame anyone either. Jessica, are you all right?"

"Mmm-hmm," Jessica said with a sniffle. She could barely stand up straight. Blasts of pain were shooting up her back.

"I'm going to go get the trainer myself," Coach said. "Jade, you help Jessica to the locker room."

"I'm okay," Jessica muttered. But Coach Laufeld was already halfway across the gym.

"Thanks a lot, Jess," Lila spat. "Why don't you stick to making yourself look bad instead of dragging the rest of us down with you?"

Jessica started crying. Their faces swam before her. She longed to run for the door, but envisioned herself slowly hobbling. She felt so pathetic.

"Lila, why don't you leave her alone?" Jade said, holding Jessica's back just as Coach had. "She's hurt."

"Yeah, Li," Melissa said, sauntering over to the little group. "You might as well teach me the stunt instead. It looks like you're going to need another stunter." She almost sounded sympathetic. Jessica wondered how she pulled it off day after day.

"So, Jessica, why don't you go lick your wounds?" Cherie asked. "There must be some guy waiting for you outside to take you back to his place anyway."

"I can't believe you dropped her!" Tia fumed at Amy and Lila as Jade walked a blubbering Jessica to the locker room.

Lila's eyes narrowed. "Excuse me?"

Tia said, "You heard me. I don't know what

103

Jessica did to you, but whatever it was, trying to physically hurt her is just sick."

"She buckled!" Amy exclaimed. "It was her fault."

"Maybe her concentration broke, but you had plenty of time to catch her. You should have had your arms cradled the second you gave the count," Tia said. She looked around at the rest of the squad. "You guys saw it."

"I saw Jessica's knees go," Cherie said. "That's all."

Tia stared at Cherie. She knew what she'd seen. And she knew she was right. "You people are un-believable."

"Tia," Melissa said in her trademark soothing voice. "It's not Lila and Amy's fault if Jessica can't handle the stunt." She rested a hand on Tia's arm, and Tia immediately batted it away. There was an audible gasp from the squad.

"Don't even try it, Melissa. You know, it wouldn't surprise me if you put them up to it."

Cherie started to step between Melissa and Tia. "Wait a minute—"

"I wasn't talking to you," Tia said. She held up a hand to Cherie and stared Melissa in the eye. "You shouldn't try to hurt Jessica just because Will has a thing for blondes."

Melissa went pale. "I can't believe you said that to me."

"That's what happened, isn't it?" Tia snapped.

104

Gina laughed. "Melissa didn't even know Laufeld was going to ask Lila and Amy to do the stunt. You're really stretching here, Tia."

Tia knew they had her there. But she also knew that Melissa had an inexplicable way of inspiring people to do really mean things for her. It was like everyone wanted to protect her and everyone wanted to be her friend. Tia had seen it all her life. Girls would do anything to get on Melissa's good side. And after what had been happening to Jessica lately, Tia could almost understand why. Melissa's bad side was not a happy place to be.

"Fine," Tia said resignedly, "but I still think Lila and Amy should apologize to Jessica."

"Yeah, right," Amy said.

Just then Coach Laufeld walked into the gym with Jade and Annie and clapped. "All right, people, the trainer is in with Jessica, so let's get back to work."

"Is she okay?" Tia asked.

"She'll be fine, but she's going to go home and get some rest for now," Coach responded.

"Guess that apology will have to wait," Lila said with a laugh.

Tia looked at the door to the locker room as the overwhelming weight of guilt by El Carro association fell on her shoulders. She had the sudden urge to go apologize to Jessica herself. Somebody had to, and it was pretty clear that none of the true offenders ever would.

"Can I just go see her?" Tia asked. She felt numerous pairs of angry and exasperated eyes turn on her.

"I appreciate your concern, Ramirez, but she's fine." Tia's heart fell. "Besides, I want you to go up next."

Great, Tia thought as Lila and Amy got back into their base positions. *I knew I should've made out my will.*

TIA RAMIREZ

NOTES FOR RESEARCH DRAFT OF SOCIOLOGY PAPER

WHEN DOES OTHER PEOPLE'S BUSINESS BECOME YOUR OWN? I MEAN, WHEN DOES A PERSON HAVE THE RIGHT TO BUTT INTO SOMEONE ELSE'S AFFAIRS? LIKE, MAYBE YOUR MOTTO IS LIVE AND LET LIVE, RIGHT? BUT HERE'S THE THING. SOMETIMES YOU HAVE TO GET INVOLVED IF YOU DON'T WANT TO FEEL LIKE A JERK.

SAY YOU SEE A LITTLE KID BEING PICKED ON BY SOMEONE A LOT BIGGER. YOU HAVE TO STEP IN, RIGHT? OR MAYBE YOU RUN ACROSS SOMEONE BEING BEAT UP. ONLY COWARDS RUN

AWAY. UNLESS, OF COURSE, THERE'S NOTHING YOU CAN DO BUT GET KILLED YOURSELF. STILL, YOU'D PROBABLY FEEL KIND OF SLEAZY RUNNING.

MAYBE IT'S ONE OF THOSE THINGS WHERE YOU JUST HAVE TO TRUST YOUR GUT REACTION. CAN YOU STAND YOURSELF IF YOU JUST WALK AWAY? (NOTE TO SELF: THIS COULD BE A GOOD PAPER. CHECK OUT STATISTICS OF PEOPLE BEING GOOD SAMARITANS—HOW MANY GOT REWARDED, HOW MANY ENDED UP GETTING SCREWED FOR IT, AND IF THEY'D DO IT AGAIN ANYWAY.)

CHAPTER 7
Everything Changes

There's nothing to be nervous about, Conner told himself as he walked into First and Ten. *Maria's cool. She'll get over it.*

He scanned the crowded restaurant and saw a hand wave. Of course Maria's eyes had been trained on the door. Should he have expected any less? Conner started to navigate the bustling room. "Where were you?" Maria asked when Conner slouched into the seat across from her.

Conner glanced at the clock over the bar—7:35. He wasn't *that* late. "I had some stuff to take care of," he said. His legs were jittering, so he pressed his palms against his thighs.

"You could have called," Maria said with a pout. "I've been sitting here for forty-five minutes."

This attitude was not helping his edginess. She was beginning to sound like his mother—or what his mom might sound like if she ever bothered to care where he was. He stretched his shoulders and gestured for the waitress, aware that Maria was growing more and more irritated with every moment he didn't respond.

The waitress appeared at the table. "Hey, Maria!" she said cheerily.

"Hi." Maria's smile was forced.

"Could we get some drinks here, babe?" Conner said.

"The name's Cary," she corrected him. But she wasn't all that annoyed. Conner could tell by the way she was eyeing him.

"Okay, then, Cary," Conner said with a half smile. "I'll have a Coke with lots of ice."

"Me too," Maria informed the waitress. Cary walked away, and Maria leaned forward in her seat, resting her palms flat on the table. "What is wrong with you?" she asked.

"Nothing." Conner shifted in his seat. It was hot in the restaurant and he was beginning to sweat, but he didn't want to take off his leather jacket. He wasn't planning on staying.

Maria's eyes flashed. "I don't get you," she said. "You call me and say you want to talk, and then you leave me waiting and don't even bother to come up with a good lie to cover it."

"So you had to entertain yourself for a few minutes—what's the big deal?" Conner looked her up and down. "No one tied you to the chair."

Maria stared at him incredulously. "I don't believe this," she said. "I thought—after last night . . ."

She took a deep breath and leaned back in her chair. Conner could practically hear her willing herself to calm down. Conner willed her to freak. It would be so much easier if she would just dump him. "I thought we were here to talk about our relationship," she said evenly.

"What's to talk about?" Conner replied, placing his hands behind his head and rocking the chair back on its rear legs. *You'll be out of here in a minute.*

"Well, are we together or aren't we?" Maria asked almost desperately.

Conner let the chair drop back to the floor. "We're together right now. Why can't you just relax and have a good time for once instead of always wanting to know exactly where you stand?"

Maria's bottom lip started to tremble. "Because that's not the way I work," she said. "I don't like being used, Conner. I *need* to know where I stand."

Conner leaned forward, gripping his hands together under the table. "I didn't tell you I wanted anything exclusive."

"That doesn't mean we'll *never* be exclusive," Maria answered. Conner was so frustrated, he wanted to punch something. Maria wasn't making this easy.

"It does to me," Conner said. "You want to know where you stand? Fine." Conner took a deep breath. "I was just having a little fun." He paused as a look of hurt shock came over Maria's face. She gaped at him, tears filling her beautiful brown eyes. Conner hated what he was about to say, but he couldn't think of any other way to make her get the point. "And I'm not having fun anymore," he said bluntly.

Maria stood up too quickly and banged her thighs on the underside of the table. She winced briefly, but managed to pull herself up straight as she yanked her handbag off the back of the chair. "I'm leaving."

"So soon?" Conner said, knowing he sounded like the biggest pig who ever lived. "Sure you won't stay for a burger?"

Tears were streaming down Maria's face, but her expression was one of defiance. "You're disgusting," she spat.

As she wove through the crowd, Conner stared at the green-tiled table and sighed.

"No arguments there."

Elizabeth looked up and almost dropped her hot cappuccino into her lap when she saw the expression on Maria's face. When she'd called fifteen minutes ago and asked Elizabeth to meet her at House of Java, Maria had sounded upset, but composed. Now, as she rushed toward Elizabeth's table at the back of the coffee shop, Maria's face was filled with panic.

"What happened?" Elizabeth asked.

"C-Conner dumped me," Maria said when she reached the table. Elizabeth's heart leaped before her brain even registered the words.

"Are you serious?" she asked. Her pulse was hammering in her ears as Maria sat down across from her. *Conner is free. Conner is free,* her mind repeated in elation. *And your best friend's heart is breaking as you sit here, you witch,* her conscience answered.

"Look at me!" Maria said, gesturing at her soaking-wet face. "Do I look serious?"

"Sorry." Elizabeth handed her a pile of napkins to use as tissues. "What happened?"

"We were supposed to talk about our relationship, where it was going," Maria explained, wiping her face clean. She took a deep breath and let it out slowly. "It's been starting to get majorly physical, and the other night I told Conner I wanted a commitment."

"And he didn't want one." Elizabeth's mind was whirling. She had known Conner wasn't serious about Maria. She had even tried to warn Maria. This shouldn't be happening.

"He said he wasn't interested in an exclusive."

"Maria, I'm so sorry," Elizabeth said truthfully. She hated seeing Maria so miserable.

"But it was the way he said it, Liz." Maria covered her mouth with her hand. Tears glistened in her eyes. "It was awful, like I meant nothing at all to him. I know you never liked him. But I really care about Conner, and tonight he made me feel like a . . . like a . . ." She broke down sobbing.

Maria had said "care," not "cared." The significance of that discrepancy wasn't lost on Elizabeth. This girl's heart was breaking wide open.

"What did he say?" Elizabeth asked. Maybe it wasn't that bad. It was possible that Maria's deep feelings for Conner had just made a polite breakup seem more harsh than it was.

"He said he was just looking for some fun," Maria said, her voice wavering. "And then he was like, 'And I'm not having fun anymore.'"

Elizabeth's heart squeezed painfully, and she slumped back in her chair. He couldn't have actually said that. She knew Conner could be rude and sarcastic, but how could he be so callous?

Elizabeth got up and put her arms around Maria.

"He doesn't deserve you," Elizabeth said firmly. She sat down in the chair next to Maria's and looked her in the eyes. "At least you found out what a loser he was before it went any further."

Maria sniffled. "I feel like such an idiot. I should have listened to you, Liz. I can't believe I freaked out on you when you tried to tell me this was going to happen. I'm so sorry."

Elizabeth's guilt quadrupled. "This is all Conner's fault," she whispered.

"I know, you're right," Maria replied. Elizabeth hadn't even realized she'd spoken out loud, but it didn't matter. She *was* right. People broke up all the time, but there was never any justification for the dumper making the dumpee feel like garbage. And that was exactly what Conner had done to Maria.

But Conner was the garbage. He was the one who deserved to have his heart smashed—if he even had one.

"Oh God, Liz!" Maria said suddenly. "You have to go back to his house! What're you going to do?"

Elizabeth smiled slyly and leaned forward in her seat. "I think I'll tell him exactly what I think of him."

"What are you doing!"

Elizabeth snatched the *Mademoiselle* magazine out of Conner's hands just as he was getting to the good part.

"I *was* reading," Conner said casually. He cocked one eyebrow. Elizabeth's face was a deep shade of red previously unknown to man. He placed his hands behind his head and leaned back into the soft couch cushions. "There was a very interesting quiz in there. So, fighting an obsession with . . . chocolate, maybe?"

Elizabeth stuffed the magazine into her shoulder bag, bending back the cover and half the pages in her fury. "How dare you go through my things!"

"Hey, you're the one who left it open on the kitchen table," Conner countered. He'd seen her miffed before, but never this over the edge. It was a little scary.

"I did not," Elizabeth said. "This was in my room. You must have gone in there!"

Conner stood up. "Not quite," he said gruffly. "Why the hell would I do that?" He expected her to back up a little when he got in her face, but she didn't. She just lifted her chin a bit higher.

"You know what? Forget it," Elizabeth said. "I don't care what you read or what you saw or what perverted things you do in your free time—"

"Perverted? What are you talking about?"

Elizabeth just continued as if he hadn't spoken. "You know why? Because I think what you did to Maria was sick. And all it proved is that you are exactly the selfish, insecure, totally inhuman poser I always thought you were."

Conner's anger was beginning to slip. It threw him off. "Hey, wait a minute—"

Elizabeth had already started to storm out of the room, but she spun around at the sound of his voice. "No, you wait a minute. Stay out of my room, stay out of my stuff, and stay away from my friends."

116

Conner followed her into the foyer. "Or you'll what?"

Elizabeth's eyes betrayed a shred of doubt. "Don't worry, I'll think of something," she said. And with that, she ran up the stairs into her room and slammed the door.

Conner fell onto the couch near the foot of the stairs. He felt like he'd just had the snot beat out of him by the class bully. Where were his comebacks? Where was his snide expression that caused all females to lose their voice in the middle of a sentence?

He rested his elbows on his knees and placed his head in his hands. Elizabeth was toeing the line here. She was somehow managing to surprise him, and that was something he wasn't used to. No one had ever taken him off guard the way Elizabeth just had.

Conner stood up and glanced at the top of the staircase. He knew she wanted him, yet she'd come in here and laced into him, knowing it could completely turn him off.

The problem was, her little self-righteous tirade had completely turned him on.

Megan Sandborn

I can't believe I'm hiding in my room. It's like when Mom and Dad used to fight, and then she'd come up here and slam the door to her room, like Elizabeth just did. It's weird. When Elizabeth and Conner were fighting, they actually sounded just like Mom and Dad, even though Elizabeth's not related to my mom, and Conner's not related to my dad.

Anyway, the other ironic thing is, I used to think my parents fighting, and their divorce, was because of me. Now, of course, I know I had nothing to do with it. They just couldn't work certain things out. Dad has managed to pound that point to death.

But this fight actually <u>was</u> my fault. Because I was the one who was

looking around Elizabeth's room. I
needed my mascara back, but then I
saw that magazine on her bed. I can
never walk away from a good issue of
<u>Mademoiselle.</u> But I didn't mean to
leave it in the kitchen.

   So what am I supposed to do now?

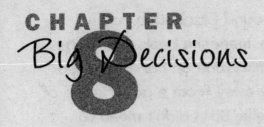

CHAPTER
Big Decisions
8

Jessica's logic had been arguing with her nerves for hours, but as the school day drew to a close on Thursday afternoon, her cartwheeling stomach won out. She couldn't handle cheerleading practice. Her lower back was still bruised, but not half as badly as her confidence. Jessica's slut status was yesterday's news. Now it was sarcastic inquiries about how her backside was doing and "spastic" jokes. She supposed she could have been glad that "Jessica Take-a-feel"—the jocks' very clever play on "Wakefield"—had faded away, but the new names were almost worse because she'd actually *done* something to deserve them.

She kept her head down as she walked quickly to her locker, but she might as well have been wearing a neon Kick Me sign. Snickers followed her down the corridor. And when she was only a few feet from her locker, an El Carro student hanging with his friends said, "Want me to kiss it better, baby?"

Forget the locker. Who needed books anyway?

Maybe she could catch Tia before practice. She had to give someone an excuse for missing practice or she'd get kicked off the squad. Tia was one of the only people who still spoke to her without a sneer in her eyes. Jessica hurried around the corner toward the row of lockers where she'd seen Tia that morning.

When Jessica cleared the bend, she caught sight of Tia standing near her locker. Jessica said a silent thank-you that there was barely anyone else around. At this point, anyone seen talking to her would probably draw jokes too. No need to drag Tia down with her.

"Tia?" Jessica said softly as she approached the locker.

Tia looked up from a scribble-covered notebook. "Hey," she said, giving Jessica a big smile. "I was just deciding whether or not I wanted to do work tonight. It's a toss-up between Spanish vocab and reruns of reruns."

Jessica felt like hugging her just for getting out two, full, insult-free sentences. "I don't take Spanish, but I have a feeling the TV is slightly more intriguing."

"A good point." She shoved the notebook into her bag. "But I might as well act responsible anyway." Tia slammed her locker shut and adjusted the strap on her backpack. "How are you feeling?"

"I'm okay. Thanks for asking." Jessica shifted

uncomfortably from one foot to the other. "But . . . uh . . . I need a favor." She half expected Tia to turn her down in a knee-jerk reaction.

But Tia smiled. "Shoot," she said, starting to walk toward the gym, obviously expecting Jessica to come with her.

Jessica pushed herself away from the lockers and stood in the middle of the hall, feeling conspicuous.

"I can't make it to cheerleading practice today. I'm just . . . it still hurts too much," she explained. She noticed her eyes were darting around out of paranoid habit, and she forced herself to look directly at Tia. She must look like a psycho. "Could you let the coach know for me?"

Tia's smile faded. "Why don't you just come to practice and watch?" she asked. "Laufeld seems like the type who would want you there unless you were dying or contagious."

Tia had no idea how right she was. Laufeld was a battle-ax when it came to missing practices and games. But Jessica was desperate, and the now familiar flutter of panic was beginning to rise in her chest.

She started backing down the hall, away from Tia. "Yeah, but I also . . . I also have to work . . . so—"

"There's no one who can cover for you?" Tia asked. Her face creased slightly, and Jessica read the pity as easily as a billboard.

Jessica shook her head and looked over her shoulder. "I tried. There's no one," she lied. "If I don't show up, I'll lose my job." She glanced at the hallway clock for effect. "I've really gotta go."

"Okay. I'll tell the coach."

"Thanks," Jessica said. "I owe you one."

Tia shrugged. "No problem."

Jessica turned and hurried toward the exit. She knew she was in for a lecture from Coach Laufeld. Last year when Sandra Bacon had broken her leg, she'd sat on the bleachers in her cheerleading sweater through the entire season. But Sandy wasn't being tormented on the side. All Jessica could think about was getting out of the school before anyone else saw her.

She'd deal with the consequences later.

Will Simmons was getting some gear from his car when Jessica ran out a side exit toward her Jeep. He quickly surveyed the parking lot. Deserted. He might not get an opportunity like this again. He threw his shoulder pads back into the trunk and started after her. Practice could wait.

"Jessica!" he called.

Jessica froze next to the Jeep, but didn't look up. He heard her start to fumble with her keys. Through the car windows he saw her face redden in desperation as she struggled to find the right key.

Will ran up to the Jeep and put his hand on the

door before she could open it. "Please, Jessica, I need to explain," he said. She didn't move—just stood there like she was waiting for the firing squad. Suddenly Will had no idea what to say. He hadn't been this close to Jessica in days. He couldn't even look at her during class or it would undoubtedly get back to Melissa, and when he'd seen her in the hall, she'd always either ducked into a bathroom or bolted in the opposite direction. Now, seeing her up close, he was drowning in self-loathing.

Jessica's hair was pulled back in a sloppy ponytail. Her clothes were baggy and drab, and there was no makeup to enhance her beautiful eyes, now tired and dull. When he'd met her, she'd been so beautiful, carefree, and fun—the type of girl a guy couldn't help looking at twice.

He'd done this to her.

"Just leave me alone," Jessica said, turning her face away.

"But I need to talk to you," Will pleaded. "I never meant for this to happen."

Jessica looked at him, her eyes full of misery tinged with anger. Will's heart dropped another notch. "What *did* you mean to happen, Will?" she said, her voice full of bitterness.

Will stared at the ground, knowing his reasons were inexcusable. Still, he had to try. "I know you hate me. And I don't blame you, but if you'd just listen to me for a second—"

"Haven't you said enough?" Jessica demanded.

It wasn't me, Will wanted to say. *I didn't start the rumors.* But it wasn't true. He had let it happen. He'd done it for Melissa. He'd just never known how far it would go.

Jessica's expression was full of disgust. "Go away, Will," she said. She loathed him. There was no denying the tone.

Will let go of the door and took a shaky step back. Jessica climbed into the car. He barely had time to jump out of the way before she slammed the Jeep into drive and screeched out of the parking lot.

"Hold on, guys!" Melissa called out as Amy and Gina started for the gym. "Coach wants to meet us in here before practice." She checked around the locker room. "I'll go tell her everyone is here."

"Jessica's not," Tia said, standing up. She hated causing any more tension on the team, but someone was going to have to start standing up to Melissa.

"I thought she wasn't going to be here today," Melissa said coolly. "Didn't you tell the coach that there was some kind of work emergency?"

Cherie laughed.

"Jessica's still on the team," Tia pointed out. "You might have mentioned that she wasn't going to be here for those of us who *hadn't* been informed."

Gina closed her locker. "Truthfully, Tia, I don't think anyone cares but you."

"I do," Annie said from the back of the room.

All right, Annie.

Cherie snorted. "Figures."

Just then Coach Laufeld stepped into the locker room. "Everyone here?" she asked Melissa.

"Except for Jessica." Melissa looked pointedly at Tia.

"Well, I want one of you to make sure she gets this information," Coach said. "The pep rally's in the gym this Saturday at eight. I want everyone there and ready to go. No excuses. Make your plans now, then I want to see you dressed and out on the gym floor in ten minutes."

The coach went into the athletic office and swung the door almost closed.

"She's in a mood," Cherie said. Tia didn't bother to point out that Coach Laufeld could still hear them. Let Cherie dig her own hole.

"Well, what do you expect, the way certain members have been neglecting the team?" Melissa said.

Tia rolled her eyes. "Can we please lay off 'certain members' for two seconds and figure out a game plan? Someone's got to make sure all the pom-poms and streamers get to the rally. And we've still got a load of banners to paint."

"I've got a bunch of paint and paper left over from last year," Melissa said.

"We have some stuff in the supply closet too," Jade said, joining the group. "We're gonna need all that red and white."

"Good point," Tia said. "Melissa, can we use your basement for painting again?"

"Sure," Melissa said. "We can meet at my house tonight to do the banners. We can even start our caravan from there on Saturday."

"What caravan?" Annie asked.

"It's an El Carro tradition," Tia told her. "All the cheerleaders go to the rally together."

"That sounds cool," Annie said.

"I think it's a great idea." Lila smiled at Melissa.

"Except for tonight," Cherie said. "I've got a paper to finish for history, and I'm way behind."

"Okay, then," Melissa said. "So Cherie—and obviously Jessica—can't make it to the banner party. The cheerleaders who *can* should meet at my house tonight at six, and all of us should be there Saturday by seven-thirty for the caravan. Everyone in agreement?" She glanced around the locker room.

"I'll let Jessica know," Tia said when no one objected.

"And you'd better tell her to actually show up for a change," Cherie advised, "or Coach *won't* be happy. "Of course the rest of us would be much happier if she *didn't* come."

Tia glanced at Coach Laufeld's office door and

smirked. Coach probably wasn't too happy right now either. Tia picked up her sneaker and yanked it on. "Don't worry about it. She'll be there."

"What's up, guys?" Elizabeth asked, coming up behind Andy and Tia on Friday morning.

"Hey, Liz," Tia said distractedly. "You sure you put *all* of them up?" she asked Andy.

"Positive," Andy said.

"Put what up?" Elizabeth asked.

"Flyers for Conner's gig," Tia said, stopping in front of her locker. "You're coming, right?"

"I don't think so, Tia," she said with a regretful tone she really didn't feel. She didn't even want to talk about Conner, let alone watch him play rock star. "It's not my scene."

"Come on, Liz, it'll be fun!" Tia shoved a flyer at her. "He's really good—wait'll you hear him."

"Oh, I've heard him," Elizabeth muttered.

"That's right!" Tia spun her lock. "I keep forgetting you guys, like, live right on top of each other." Elizabeth blushed at the mental image. "Does he practice a lot?" Tia asked.

"It depends on what you call 'a lot.'" Elizabeth leaned back against the locker next to Tia's. "Before school, after school, through dinner, weekends—"

"Good!" Tia said. "He keeps trying to tell me he doesn't care, but I knew he was lying."

Elizabeth glanced at the ridiculous flyer as Tia

made Andy list all the places he'd posted them around town. Conner looked like a Martian from a bad 1950s sci-fi flick.

She fought not to laugh. God, the audacity of the guy! *"Live,"* like he was some superstar with videos and CDs filling record stores across the country. She could just imagine what his gig would be like—him playing third-rate covers of old Doors tunes and waiting for the girls to drool.

"I've really got a lot of work to do on the *Oracle,*" Elizabeth lied. "It's pretty impossible."

"It's only a couple of hours," Tia insisted. She checked her lipstick in her locker mirror and wiped her fingers down the sides of her mouth. "And I really want you to come."

"Yeah," Andy said. "I can pick you up."

Elizabeth stared at her shoes. She couldn't tell Tia and Andy what she really thought of Conner. For whatever reason, they both considered the slimeball to be one of their best friends. But she'd been giving him the ice-girl treatment since last night, and going to see him play might just undo her progress. Besides, she didn't want him thinking she supported him or something.

"Come on, Liz," Tia prodded, slamming her locker door and handing her books to Andy. "It won't be the same without you."

"Really?" Elizabeth was flattered. "I don't know. . . ."

"*Please*," Tia begged. "I'll have such a better time if you're there."

Andy shot Tia an irritated look and shoved her books back into her hands. "On behalf of Angel and me, thanks."

Tia and Elizabeth laughed. "You know what I mean, Andy," Tia said.

"Okay, maybe," Elizabeth said. "But I'm not making any promises." That should satisfy Tia for at least a few minutes.

"Good enough," Tia said. She glanced at her watch. "Oooh, come on, Andy. I've gotta copy your history notes before class."

As her friends hurried away, Elizabeth checked out the flyer again. *Yeah, why not?* she thought. She'd have a good time hanging out with Tia and Andy. And she'd have the added bonus of watching Conner fall flat on his face.

Jessica Wakefield

For a while there, I was thinking how great it would be not to feel anything — to be one of those people who doesn't care what anyone thinks. Like all those nerds I used to laugh at who dress like they're color blind <u>and</u> pattern blind and pore over <u>X-Files</u> books during their lunch periods. They never care who's laughing.

But not caring and not feeling are two different things. Not caring just means you have enough confidence to ignore others' opinions. Not feeling, well, even if it might be painless, it would be kind of un-human.

After what happened at the last practice, I was seriously considering skipping the pep rally and dropping off the team. It seemed like all I was doing was letting myself get beaten up over and over again. Like I wasn't getting enough torture during the day, so I had to spend three hours at practice every day and get some more. I didn't want to feel like a loser anymore. I didn't want to feel like I'd lost everything. I was <u>this</u> <u>close</u> to walking into Laufeld's office and bagging it.

But that changed when I saw Will Simmons. Will made me feel something else yesterday — anger. I never knew how productive anger could be.

It still hurts — nothing has changed there. But I'm determined to show the school I don't care what they think of me. I'm going to that pep rally if I have to crawl. It doesn't matter if they drop me, boo me, or throw tomatoes at me. They're not going to make me forget who I am. Not <u>was</u>, am.

And oh, yeah, just so it's in writing, I swear I will never laugh at a nerd again.

CHAPTER
The Best Intentions

Will looked at his watch for the tenth time in as many minutes and exhaled loudly. Where was she? Melissa had told him she'd meet him outside the girls' locker room at six-thirty, and it was already six forty-five. The pep rally was coming up, so cheerleading practices had the tendency to run long, but most of the squad had left over fifteen minutes ago.

He waited five more minutes, then walked up to the locker-room door. He only hesitated for a second. If he didn't get something into his stomach soon, he was going to wither and die.

Will pushed open the door, but kept his back to the room. He started to call Melissa's name, but stopped when he heard her voice. Maybe she was on her way out.

"So, you tell everyone but her that we're meeting at the auxiliary gym at seven-thirty instead of my house," Melissa was saying in a confidential tone. "By the time she figures it out, the pep rally will have already started."

"What about the banners and stuff?" Will recognized Cherie's voice.

"Don't worry." Melissa again. "I asked my mom if I could borrow the Explorer. Everything will fit in there."

Will eased the door closed. Jessica. He knew they were talking about Jessica. Melissa was actually plotting to make her miss the pep rally. Will leaned back against the cool brick wall, his heart pounding. If Jessica missed the pep rally, there was no doubt in his mind that she'd get thrown off the squad.

Will paced the hall. He should confront Cherie and Melissa—tell them to drop it.

"Yeah, right," Will muttered. "Melissa will love that." He punched his fist into a locker and barely felt it. He had to do something. Jessica didn't deserve this.

But what? He glanced at the pay phone. Would she even talk to him if he called? Probably not. Then it hit him. A note! He could jot down what he knew and leave it in Jessica's locker.

He glanced at his watch. Melissa had kept him waiting. Now he could return the favor.

Will jogged down the hall and took a right at the science lab. Jessica's locker was the third on the right. Yanking open his backpack, he ripped a piece of paper from his sociology notebook.

135

Jessica—

There's been a change of plans for the pep rally. They're meeting at the auxiliary gym at seven-thirty, not Melissa's house. Trust me. Don't go to Melissa's.

Will

Will read it over, then crossed out his name and scribbled over it until it was totally illegible. There was no way Jessica was going to trust him. He just had to hope she'd trust an anonymous friend.

Will folded the paper and was about to shove it through one of the slats in the locker door when Josh Radinsky, Matt Wells, and Seth Hiller came around the corner, freshly showered from football practice.

Will shoved the note into his jeans pocket and stretched.

"What's up, man?" Seth asked.

"Nothing much." Will faked a yawn. "Just wandering the halls."

Josh glanced toward Jessica's locker. "Yeah?"

"What are you guys up to?" Will said before Josh could put two and two together. As if the guy was capable.

Matt grinned. "We're goin' to First and Ten for a burger. You in?"

"Sorry, I promised Melissa I'd take her and Cherie out for a pizza. They're meeting me up here." *Go away,* Will urged. The note was burning a hole in his pocket.

"Pizza?" Matt looked at the other guys. "What do you guys think?"

"I'll take pizza with that Reese babe over burgers with you doofs any day," Seth said.

Josh whacked Seth's arm, but shrugged. "I'm in."

Will searched for some excuse to get rid of his friends, but came up empty. If he hadn't mentioned Cherie, he could have claimed it was a date. But now it was a flirt-with-Cherie free-for-all.

"Come on," Matt said, throwing his arm around Will. "Can't keep the ladies waiting."

"I have to go to my locker," Will said, pulling away. "I'll catch up."

"All right, man," Josh said.

Will waited until the guys were around the corner. He yanked out the note and stuffed it into Jessica's locker in one quick motion.

Then he took a step back and frowned. "At least I tried."

Tia was getting ready to head to the House of Java for Conner's big premiere when the phone

137

rang. "Tia!" her brother Miguel called from the hallway. "It's for you!"

Tia laid her brush down on her bureau. "Who is it?" she called.

"Beats me!" Miguel called back, loud enough for whoever it was on the other end of the phone to hear. "Some girl, that's all I know."

"What girl?" Tia said, rushing down the hall. "Twelve years old and you still don't know how to answer the phone right," she admonished Miguel, faking a slap to his head when she reached the phone.

Miguel shrugged. "You pick it up and say hello. What's to know?" he replied. He ran out of the house, bouncing a basketball in front of him.

Tia shook her head in exasperation and picked up the receiver, which was lying on the table. "Hello?" she said.

"Tia? It's Cherie."

"Hey," Tia said, totally taken aback. What could Cherie possibly be calling her about on a Friday night? Except for cheerleading, they had absolutely nothing in common. "What's up?"

"I just called to let you know that we're going to be meeting at the auxiliary gym at seven-thirty instead of Melissa's house tomorrow. Her mother's having a party and doesn't want our cars crowding the driveway. Melissa's going to take all the stuff to the rally in her car, and we're just going to forget the caravan this time."

Great. One more El Carro tradition down the tubes. "It's too bad we didn't know about this sooner," Tia said, not bothering to mask her disappointment. "We could have left the stuff at my house and gone from here together."

"Uh-huh," Cherie said. "I guess it slipped Melissa's mind. You know how it is."

Not really. The only parties Tia's parents had were for the kids' birthdays, and no one ever forgot those. "Should I call anyone?" Tia asked. "I mean, is there anyone you haven't told yet?"

There was a short pause on the other end. "Not that I can think of," Cherie said finally. "I mean, I've called practically everyone else already."

"Jessica?" Tia asked skeptically.

"Yeah, well, I told Lila, and they live together, so . . . you know."

Tia's eyes narrowed. "So I know what?"

"Well, of course Lila's going to *tell* her," Cherie said, like Tia was a total moron.

Tia took a deep breath. "But did you *tell* Lila to tell her? Because in case you haven't noticed, those two aren't exactly talking."

"She said she'd pass along the message," Cherie said, sounding exasperated. "Satisfied?"

"All right," Tia said. "Thanks for calling."

"Of course."

Tia made a gagging motion with her finger, then hung up the phone.

She glanced at her watch. If she didn't get going soon, she'd miss Conner's opening song. Angel was going to be here any minute, and she hadn't even finished doing her hair yet!

Conner straightened his leather jacket and checked his hair in the House of Java's bathroom mirror. His hands were fluttering, so he shook them out violently and took a deep breath. He'd had to walk through the crowd to get to the rest room. Everyone in Sweet Valley and El Carro had turned out to watch him crash and burn. Those flyers of Tia's were everywhere and, according to Andy, she'd managed to verbally harass anyone who had even dared say they couldn't make it tonight.

"Well, if you're gonna bomb, might as well go nuclear," Conner told his reflection.

Conner reached into his pocket and squeezed his good-luck charm—a pick Gavin had given him that he swore was touched by Jerry Garcia. Conner wasn't sure if he believed his guitar teacher, but it was comforting anyway. He nodded once at himself, then headed to the small, cobblestone courtyard out back. It was still early, but he couldn't handle talking to himself like a lunatic for one more second.

Conner had been to performances here plenty of times, so he knew what to expect—the white Christmas lights decorating the bushes that edged the courtyard, the cozy candlelit tables, and especially the stage set up at the right of the courtyard. What he hadn't expected was to see that the crowd had doubled while he was in the bathroom. He made a mental note to kill Tia before the night was over.

Conner managed not to gawk at the audience as he moved to the stage to set up his gear. Within seconds Jack Leary, the manager who was in charge of hiring the acts, walked over to Conner and placed a hand on Conner's shoulder. "I know you're not slated to start until eight," he said. "But there's a pretty big crowd here already. I'll throw you an extra ten if you start at seven-thirty."

Conner's heart took a nosedive, but he managed a casual shrug. "Sure," he said. *The sooner you start, the sooner it's over,* he reminded himself. Then he realized his mouth was void of moisture. "Could you get me some water?" he whispered.

"Sure, man."

Conner slung his guitar strap over his shoulder, sat down on the stool, and pulled the mike down to his mouth. Jack showed up with the water. Conner thanked him, downed the drink,

141

and placed the glass on top of his amp. Then he bit the bullet and looked up.

Every table was full. Conner saw Megan grinning at him and knew she was sitting on her hands to keep from waving and embarrassing him. His friend Evan and a few other guys were in the back corner, sipping java, totally oblivious to the fact that Conner was onstage. And right smack in the middle of the crowd, sitting with Tia, Angel, and Andy, was Elizabeth.

When she caught him looking at her, she yawned and looked around the audience like she was as bored as a stoplight on a dead-end street.

Conner dropped his gaze and tugged nervously at the sleeves of his jacket. Tia had told him Elizabeth probably wouldn't show because she had too much work to do on the *Oracle*. Conner had smiled to himself when Tia said that. He'd heard Elizabeth on the phone often enough using that editor's job of hers as an excuse for not doing something she didn't want to. He wondered what had made her change her mind tonight.

She was probably here to gloat. She knew he'd been practicing his ass off, and now she was here to watch him suck. He began to tune his guitar and felt himself smiling.

He'd show her.

Conner winked at Megan, then he leaned into

the mike. "This first song is called 'Jimi's Way,'" he said to the audience. "A tribute to the great Jimi Hendrix."

Elizabeth looked at him, a smug smile on her face. He gave her a little nod, then positioned his fingers and started to play.

Conner's nerves melted away as his fingers started to move. He found himself closing his eyes and concentrating on nothing but the music, just like he did when he was up in his room. When he'd made it halfway through the song, he remembered to look at the audience, and it only caught him off guard for a moment. He felt nothing but the strings beneath his fingertips and the chords vibrating through his bones.

Conner languidly strummed the last chord and barely heard the audience applaud before he went right into his next song. By the time he'd hit the third tune, he knew he had them. The entire audience was hanging on every note—no talking, no ordering cappuccinos. Before he knew it, he'd reached the end of his set.

"I call this final tune 'Stone Heart.'"

For the first time since he started, he glanced at Elizabeth. The smugness was gone. When she saw him watching her, she swallowed hard and glanced away. Conner smiled.

He kept his eyes on her as he began to play.

*　　　*　　　*

You catch a glimpse of sun-streaked hair
Flashing 'cross the room,
She's hotter 'n Santa Ana winds,
Cool as iced perfume.

And you'd tell her what you're feelin'
But can't break your golden rule,
Keep yourself from bein' hurt, man,
Keep your stone heart cool.

She's reachin' for your soul, boy,
But you know that hard-fast rule,
She'll wrap you up too tight, now,
Keep your stone heart cool.

Conner's heart was pounding as he played, and he could barely believe he was getting the words out. Elizabeth's gaze never wavered. She didn't look away in embarrassment. She didn't fake a cough so she could avert her eyes. She might have been breathing a little heavier, but she wasn't going to let him win.

As the last chord faded away, Conner felt himself coming down from an incredible high. Elizabeth had never looked as beautiful as she did at that moment—all flushed and glassy-eyed in the soft light. He had never wanted to be alone with anyone so badly.

Suddenly a loud roar of applause broke out,

and Conner was slammed back to reality. He tore his gaze away from Elizabeth. What was he thinking? *It was just the music,* he told himself. *Just the rush of performing for an audience.* But he knew it was more than that. It was Elizabeth—her innocence, her bravery, her damn hair—everything that had inspired the song.

Conner forced himself to acknowledge the applause and whistles. When it finally died down and people started to leave, Conner stepped into the audience, trying hard not to look in Elizabeth's direction. A cute girl with short black hair, wearing a bomber's jacket and faded jeans, came up to him. "I'm Judy," she said, flashing him a smile. "That was amazing."

"Thanks," Conner said, trying not to show his surprise as several other girls rushed over and introduced themselves. He knew it was the whole musician mystique they were into more than his music, but it felt good. When a couple of guys came up to shake his hand, Conner was surprised. For guys to bother talking to him, he *must've* been good.

Conner saw Tia pushing through the crowd and waved. She ran up to him and threw her arms around him. "I don't even know what to say!" she squealed, a huge smile lighting her face. "Except you should have done this a lot sooner."

"Seriously, man," Angel said, flashing his easy

grin. "Better start practicing that autograph."

Megan rushed up and grabbed him around the waist. "My brother, the rock star." She was beaming, and Conner ran a hand over her shiny red-blond hair. "I just thought you should know that any of my friends who weren't previously in love with you are now."

Conner looked back toward Megan's table, where a bunch of sophomores were gawking and giggling.

"I'll keep that in mind," he said with a laugh. Megan swatted his arm and ran back to her friends.

"Totally cool, man," Andy said, raising his hand for a high five.

As Conner slapped Andy's palm, he noticed that Elizabeth was watching him from across the courtyard. He raised his eyes to hers. This time she looked away. Conner tried to focus on Andy, but his eyes wandered back to her again. She really looked good tonight—not just the short brown skirt and tightish white T-shirt. But the glow to her complexion, the sparkle to her eyes . . .

She met his gaze again and didn't flinch. Conner's heart skipped a beat. This was insane. This felt like—

"So where do you want to go to celebrate?" Tia asked Conner.

"How about Crescent Beach?" Angel suggested.

Conner barely heard them. His eyes were searching Elizabeth's, wondering what she was thinking.

"Or we could maybe check out the Riot if you want someplace with music," Tia said. "What do you think?"

Elizabeth's hair shimmered like muted gold in the Christmas lights. He knew it would feel like silk if he touched it.

"Conner?"

Conner took a step toward Elizabeth.

"Conner!"

"What?" Conner pulled himself back. Tia was practically screaming in his ear.

"What do you want to *do*?" Tia demanded in an exasperated tone.

"Do?" Conner glanced at Elizabeth. She turned to gather up her bag and jacket. "Uh . . . I was thinking of going home."

Elizabeth froze. Her back was to him, but he knew she'd heard him.

"Home? But you just finished your first gig," Tia protested, walking through the thinning crowd toward the table where Elizabeth was standing. She turned around slowly as they approached. "You're supposed to celebrate," Tia added.

Andy nodded in agreement. "Real musicians don't wander home till at least three or four in the morning. I think we should do the Riot."

Conner stared at Elizabeth. They were right. He should celebrate. Besides, Conner would never hear the end of it if he didn't. But Elizabeth—

"Are you coming, Liz?" Tia asked.

She glanced at Tia and smiled apologetically. "I don't think so," she said. "I really should get home and do some of that work I've been avoiding all night."

"I'll drive you," Conner blurted out. *God, had he just said that?*

Elizabeth looked as surprised as Conner felt. "But aren't you—"

Conner looked at Tia. "I want to drop off my guitar, so I'll meet you at the Riot, okay?"

"Okay," Tia said, her eyes darting between Elizabeth and Conner as if she was waiting for one of them to explode. "See you tomorrow, Liz."

What am I doing? Conner wondered, watching Andy, Angel, and Tia walk away.

Elizabeth cleared her throat, and Conner realized he'd been standing there second-guessing himself while she waited.

"So—"

"I gotta get my guitar," he said. He started for the stage, hoping he was acting a lot cooler than he felt.

Maria Slater

There's a school of thought that if you want something bad enough and if you project that desire into the universe, eventually you'll get it. Energy is energy whether it's physical or mental. Eventually that energy takes form.

I know the theory's way out there, but I have two choices. I can continue feeling miserable and hopeless about losing Conner (like I did all night while my friends were at HOJ watching him play), or I can try to get him back without pushing him further away. So here goes.

I want Conner to realize he loves me. Maybe he'll see me with another guy or run into someone who reminds him of me. However it happens, I want him to understand he's totally unhappy without me.

I want him to beg me to come back to him,

although I don't plan to give in too fast. He needs to suffer a little. And to send me dozens and dozens of roses. Color optional.

After a long, passionate reunion we'll be a couple, and all my friends will envy what a wonderful relationship I have.

Okay, there it is. I'm sending it out.

I know it's kind of crazy, but I'm feeling better already, just believing there's a chance.

CHAPTER 10
All About Control

Elizabeth was having a minor nervous breakdown while Conner packed up his stuff. She couldn't believe she'd accepted a ride from him, but the yes had just come out of her mouth. Yesterday she'd been full of the most potent anger she'd ever experienced, and now . . . now her heart was pounding faster than ever.

"I'm gonna go wait out front," Elizabeth said as Conner bent to unplug his guitar.

"Fine," he said without turning around.

Elizabeth practically ran through the café and out the front door. She sat on one of the green-slated benches on the sidewalk and tried to compose herself. Something had happened during Conner's set. She was more sure than ever that a lot of Conner's tough act was a front to hide his insecurities. No one could write lyrics that touching if he was totally callous.

But why did he have to be so cruel to Maria? She could understand wanting to keep people at arm's length. A lot of people had that attitude. But that wasn't what he'd done with Maria. He'd pretty much obliterated any chance of even having a conversation with the girl ever again.

It made no sense. Conner had been so charming, so talented, so full of emotion. There was a depth there that she'd never seen before, the sensitivity of an artist, not the cockiness of a guy faking his way through adequate imitation. And that final song, about a guy scared of being hurt— Elizabeth shuddered as she remembered the way she'd felt with Conner's penetrating eyes locked on hers.

Elizabeth glanced through the window behind her, but couldn't see anything other than muted shadows bent over cups of steaming coffee. She sighed, knowing that when Conner finally walked through the door, his armor would be back in place. He wasn't going to look at her like that again—like she was all he could see. She had to put aside the thought that was tugging at the far reaches of her mind—that Conner had finally decided she was worth getting to know.

The door swung open and the bells jangled loudly.

Conner looked right, then left, and saw her. "Hey," he said, stuffing his free hand in his pocket.

Elizabeth took a deep breath of the cool night air, sweet with the aroma of French roast and freshly mowed lawn. "Hey."

"The car's over there." He gestured over his shoulder. "Ready?"

Elizabeth stood. *Ready for what, exactly?* she wondered. As she followed Conner to his car, a warm breeze lifted the hair off the back of her neck. There was an unreal quality to the night, as if she were walking in a dream. Conner opened the car door for her, then went around to the other side of the Mustang. The interior light went out when he closed the door, leaving them in a soft darkness lit only by dim street lamps and a three-quarter moon.

Conner started the car. Elizabeth knew better than to expect any conversation. Inside, she was dying to ask him why he'd offered her a ride. It wasn't like Conner had a history of considerate behavior. Andy would have gladly taken her home, and Conner knew it.

Conner reached over and flicked on the radio, then ran his hand through his hair and blew out a burst of breath. Elizabeth watched him out of the corner of her eye and realized in a rush that he was actually nervous. Somehow that made her more comfortable. She leaned back in her seat and tried not to smile. For once she wasn't the one sweating it.

Conner pulled into the driveway and killed the engine. The silence was deafening.

"Are you going to tell me what you thought?"

The sudden sound of his voice sent her heart racing in the darkness.

"Thought?" she repeated.

"Of the set." Conner was looking through the windshield at the garage.

Elizabeth was at a loss for words. She had a feeling Conner would take anything she said and put it under a magnifying glass—scrutinizing it until he squeezed out every possible ounce of subtext. Then, mercifully, the words he'd once graced her with popped into her head.

She turned toward him, and he glanced over. "Moving," she said. "Surprisingly moving."

Conner just looked at her for a moment, and she had the mortifying sensation that he didn't remember the reference.

And then he laughed. And it wasn't a snide laugh or a mocking one. It was the first real, genuine, heartfelt expression he'd ever shared in her presence. Elizabeth grinned.

When he stopped, he sighed audibly and popped his seat belt. Elizabeth thought he was about to get out of the car, but instead he turned to face her. His eyes looked almost gray in the soft light. All Elizabeth could hear was his breathing, her breathing, her rushing pulse.

Kiss me, Elizabeth thought. *Kiss me. Kiss me. Kiss me.*

There was nothing and no one else in the world.

Conner leaned toward her, pulling her deep inside his intense eyes. Her eyelids half-closed, waiting for their lips to meet. Waiting for his hand to touch her cheek.

He lifted his arm. Elizabeth couldn't breathe. His arm was around her now, warm and strong—

And then she heard the door pop open—felt the cool rush of air against her back.

Elizabeth's eyes flicked open, and Conner fell back into his seat.

"Trick handle, remember?" he said.

Elizabeth's whole body turned into a puddle at his feet. How could she have let him do this to her again? After a moment of complete loss of motor ability, Elizabeth managed to pull herself out of the car and slammed the door.

"Thanks for the ride," she said, trying to cover. But her words were drowned out by the revving engine. Before she could even breathe again, Conner had peeled out of the driveway, leaving her behind in a cloud of dust and exhaust.

"What a night." Conner groaned as he flopped into bed, fully clothed. His friends had dragged him from the Riot to Crescent Beach. Then he'd driven around for over an hour, too wired to even think of sleep.

Switching off the bedside lamp, Conner closed his eyes and exhaled deeply. But two seconds later he was staring at the ceiling. All the excitement had obviously gotten to him. He'd already gone over the gig a hundred times, but he let his mind wander back. Everyone had said he was good, so Conner supposed it was true. Good enough for House of Java anyway. Whatever that meant.

He could still feel the high of playing in front of an appreciative audience. He could see the girls swarming around him after the show, the guys shaking his hand. Tia . . . Andy . . . Angel . . . Elizabeth . . .

He sat up straight in bed. He was not going to allow his mind to go there. Not again. He pressed his palms against his forehead. It had been happening all night. That Judy chick had found him at the Riot and pressed her number into his hand. Two seconds later he'd been wondering what Elizabeth was doing—whether she was mad he hadn't kissed her. It was so obvious she wanted him to.

The sexual tension in the car had been so heavy, he could feel it pressing on every inch of his body. She had wanted him to kiss her. Bad.

And he almost did. Leaning across her like that—it wasn't to get the door. But when he was so close he could almost taste her, he realized he couldn't do it—not to Elizabeth. He knew that if he kissed her, he might not want to stop. Eventually it would just end the same way it had

156

ended with Maria, and he couldn't have that.

"Get a grip, Conner," he told himself, lying back down against the cool pillow. "You don't need more drama. You definitely don't need it."

His heart started to return to its normal pace, and Conner smiled to himself. He was fine. Sooner or later, Elizabeth would be out of his house and he wouldn't constantly have to see her, hear her, smell her. He could control himself until then. It was all about control, and Conner had never had a problem with that before.

Then he heard a squeak, and his eyes popped open again. Another squeak. What was that? A third, and his heart slammed into his rib cage.

It was Elizabeth's bed. She was turning in her sleep.

This is so not good, he thought. He and Elizabeth were only a few inches apart. If the wall disappeared, he could reach out and touch her. *No you couldn't, idiot,* he thought. *Her bed's on the other side of the room.* But still . . . .

He found himself lying very still, straining to hear any sound from the next room. He imagined Elizabeth lying there, her long legs deeply tan against the yellow sheets, her blond hair spread across the pillow. . . .

The bed squeaked again and Conner pictured Elizabeth in those baby-doll pajamas, the ones she had on when he surprised her in the kitchen a while back and she dropped the glass of milk. He could still see her stooping to pick up the broken pieces, not realizing what a view he was getting until it was too late.

He turned over onto his stomach. Enough. He had to get some sleep. But he kept seeing that nightgown, and the fire in Elizabeth's eyes when she told him off about Maria. He could even smell the perfume she wore—sweet but subtle. Ridiculously enticing. Conner closed his eyes, but knew it was futile.

And to think, she was only a few feet away. . . .

Jessica Wakefield

My Wish List

I wish the earthquake never happened and Melissa Fox and Will Simmons had stayed in El Carro.

I wish I lived anywhere but with the Fowlers.

I wish I had so many friends, I'd need three huge address books for all their numbers.

I wish I was famous and everyone who ever hurt me was totally mortified they lost me as a friend.

I wish I could erase every bad thing that's happened this school year from everyone's memory.

But mostly, I wish this pep rally thing will work.

"Where's Jessica?" Tia asked, approaching the dance bar in the auxiliary gym, where Cherie was stretching. It was seven forty-two and everyone else was there already.

Cherie straightened up and began to rotate her shoulders. "Where do you think?" she said.

Tia glanced around the gym. Gina, Amy, and Renee were all obviously listening in and pretending they weren't. Melissa, Annie, Lila, and Jade were outside, unloading the banners from Melissa's car. "I don't *know* what to think," she replied. "That's why I'm asking you."

"Maybe you should be asking Lila," Cherie said, lightly placing her hands on her hips. "She's the one who was supposed to tell her." Tia heard Gina stifle a giggle.

Tia's heart dropped. There was something going on here. "You never told Lila to tell her, did you?"

"God, are you her new best friend or what?" Cherie asked, readjusting the barrette holding back her hair. She had an annoyed look on her

160

face. "It's not like Jessica hasn't missed practices in the past."

"This isn't a practice," Tia pointed out. She looked at the clock. "The rally starts soon."

Cherie shrugged. "All right, then. Last I heard, she was sick."

"True, but where *is* she?" Gina quipped, earning a round of laughter from the rest of the squad.

"Why didn't you say that in the first place?" Tia asked. She didn't like the feel of this. The back of her neck was starting to prickle with sweat.

Cherie flashed her a wry smile. "I guess it slipped my mind," she said. "Shouldn't you be warming up?" She glanced at the door as Melissa and the others walked in and dropped the banners on the floor.

Tia marched over to Lila and pulled her out of the gym so they wouldn't have an audience.

"What are you doing?" Lila screeched, shaking her off.

"Where's Jessica?" Tia asked.

"I don't know," Lila answered, irritated. "I'm not her keeper."

"But she's not sick?" Tia said.

"Not that I know of," Lila said. "She was working this afternoon, I think." Her eyes narrowed slightly. "What's going on?"

"Did Cherie ever tell you to tell Jessica that the

meeting place was changed tonight?" Tia asked.

Lila crossed her arms over her chest. "No," she said slowly. "She told me you were going to tell her." Lila's complexion waned a bit. "Wait a minute—"

"Come on, ladies!" Coach Laufeld walked into the lobby from the direction of the athletic office. She nudged Lila and Tia back into the gym and followed behind them, clapping. "Get in formation. I want to see the hello cheer."

Lila shot Cherie a scathing look and shuffled into the center of the room. Tia saw Melissa and Cherie glance at each other worriedly, obviously wondering what Lila had told Tia. When everyone was lined up, Coach Laufeld studied their lines. Tia swallowed back her panic as she waited for the inevitable. *Walk through that door, Jessica. Please.*

"Where's Wakefield?" Coach asked in a resigned voice.

"She's sick," Tia said, before anyone else could tell the coach that Jessica was just blowing off the rally. "Her sister told me she spent half the day at the doctor."

"That's too bad," Coach Laufeld said. "But I have to say, you've had just as much practice time without her as you have with her, so you should be fine out there."

Tia could just feel Melissa and her friends' triumphant grins behind her back. Cherie had lied to her, and she knew Melissa had been in on it. She'd even lied to Lila, and Tia had thought those three were becoming friends. Now Jessica was going to miss the pep rally and Tia could have prevented it. Why hadn't she seen this coming?

Jessica pulled the Jeep to a stop in front of Melissa's house and let the engine idle for a minute. The place was deserted. There wasn't a single car in the driveway. She'd had trouble finding her way there and had lost five or ten minutes on wrong turns. But it was only seven thirty-five. She fought the sick feeling twisting her stomach and climbed out of the car. Maybe the squad had parked their cars around the corner or something.

It took forever for someone to answer the bell. Jessica was about to ring again when a woman with Melissa's clear blue eyes and delicate features opened the door. She glanced at Jessica's uniform, and a shadow of confusion crossed her face. "Can I help you?" she asked.

"Mrs. Fox?" Jessica said.

"Yes."

"I'm on the cheerleading squad," Jessica blurted. "Is the rest of the team here?"

"Here? No. I'm sorry, dear," Mrs. Fox said kindly. "Melissa left a half hour ago. She told me she was meeting the team at school."

Jessica's knees went weak, and she grabbed onto the porch railing for support.

"Are you all right?" Mrs. Fox asked.

"Sorry to bother you," Jessica whispered. She swallowed against the tightness in her throat. Mrs. Fox smiled sympathetically. "What's the easiest way back to Sweet Valley?" After the trouble she'd had getting there, she'd been hoping she could follow some of the other girls back.

"Take a right out of the driveway and a left onto Pacific Way. Pacific will fork into 119. You want to pass 119 and take a right onto 11A. Take that west to Ocean Drive and then head north," Mrs. Fox told her.

"Thanks." She turned slowly and then ran for her car. Tia's words rang in her ears. *Be at Melissa's at seven-thirty sharp*, she had said. *And Jess, please be on time. The coach is pretty upset that you've been missing practice.*

She had to have heard right. "Seven-thirty at the school" couldn't exactly be mistaken for "seven-thirty at Melissa's."

Jessica revved the engine and checked the clock. The pep rally started in twenty minutes. She had to concentrate on remembering the directions. Any wrong turns and she was fried.

Her hands were shaking as she hit the road. *Please let me get there in time,* she prayed as she came to the end of Melissa's street. Pacific Way. Take a left here.

But when she came to the fork in the road, she couldn't remember what Mrs. Fox had said. Something about 119. Take 119 west?

Tears spilled over onto Jessica's cheeks. She turned right onto 119. But after a couple of miles, she saw a sign for La Mesa through her tears. La Mesa was south of El Carro, and she needed to be heading north.

Part of her just wanted to find Sweet Valley and go home. She'd never make it in time now anyway. But then she remembered the promise she'd made herself, that she'd get through the pep rally no matter what. Jessica wiped the tears from her eyes with the back of her hand. She had to get to the high school. She couldn't break down now.

Making a U-turn, she sped back the way she had come, passing cars, trucks, anything that moved too slowly for her—which at this point was everything on the road. It was eight-eleven when she finally pulled into the Sweet Valley High parking lot. The lot was packed. Maybe she still had a chance. These things never started on time.

Frantic, Jessica sped up the hill to the lot behind the school and swung the Jeep into the first space she saw. She raced toward the gym, spurred by the sound of faint cheers floating into the still air outside. They'd already started.

She was breathing hard by the time she reached

the back of the gym. She yanked hard on the door. Locked.

"No!" she wailed out loud, sure that no one could possibly hear her over the music and the cheering. She banged against the metal door. "Someone let me in!" she yelled. But it was useless.

Desperate, she ran around to the front of the gym. This time the door flew open when she yanked on the handle. She was standing right next to the packed bleachers. Everyone was focused on the court, so Jessica inconspicuously inched along the wall toward the front of the bleachers. *Calm down, calm down,* she told herself as she walked. Then over the loudspeaker she heard the coach say, "And last but not least—Tia Ramirez!"

Jessica came to a dead stop. A couple of teachers were blocking her view of the court, but it didn't matter. The coach had said "last but not least." That meant the whole team had already been called. She was too late. The tears that she'd been fighting broke loose, spilling onto her cheeks as the crowd cheered for Tia. It was worse than anything she had imagined. She never even had a chance.

Will was standing against the wall in the back-right corner of the gym, near the door that attached the gym to the rest of the school. He had maneuvered his way to this end of the line on purpose so that he could keep an eye on the door. But Jessica had never shown up, and now the cheerleaders were all out on the court.

She never found the note, Will thought, pulling at the collar of his brand-new, red-and-white varsity jacket. *I should have warned her. I should have known she wouldn't see that scrap of paper. I should have gone to her house and made her listen to me.*

"Hey, man." Todd Wilkins nudged Will's elbow to get his attention. "Check it out."

Will followed Todd's gaze, and his heart skipped a beat. Jessica was hovering next to the bleachers by the far wall, and the sight of her nearly tore his heart out.

"She looks like hell," Wilkins said. "Maybe we should tell somebody."

But Will barely heard him. "Outta the way, man," he said, pushing Todd forward. Will walked behind his team along the wall, racing toward the bleachers. When he got there, he was going to have to walk in front of the crowd, in front of the cheerleaders and Melissa and everyone, but at that moment he didn't care.

He had to tell her he was sorry—that everything was going to be okay. But when he got to the end of the line, she suddenly turned and ran out the door. Will felt a hand on his shoulder.

"Where the hell are you going, Will?"

"Josh, leave me alone," Will said, turning around to face his friend.

"You're going after her? Are you nuts?" Josh asked. "Melissa will kill you, man."

"I don't care," Will said vehemently.

He pushed open the back door of the gym just as Jessica ran past, heading for the back parking lot.

"Jessica!" Will yelled. The gym door slammed shut behind him, the noise lost among the cheers.

Jessica stopped and slowly turned around. She was convulsing with sobs, but when she saw Will, she turned again and started stumbling up the hill.

Will easily caught up with her. This time he was going to make her listen to him. He grabbed her arm.

"Why can't you just leave me alone?" she asked, her voice cracking as she looked away.

Will's heart turned. "Because." He paused, searching for the words that would make her stay. He could only think of two. "I'm sorry."

Jessica glared at him through tear-filled eyes. "You're sorry. For what?" she asked. "For lying to me? For making me care about you? For telling everyone I was a slut? Or for having a psychotic girlfriend whose sole purpose in life is to ruin mine?"

Will let her go and looked at the ground. He'd

hurt her so deeply, and he knew now that he could never make any of it go away. He could never take back the pain he'd caused Jessica *or* Melissa.

He took a deep breath and looked her directly in the eye. "For everything," he said. "I wish I could take it all back, but I can't." He reached out tentatively and took her wrist. She was shaking, but she didn't pull away. His heart was pounding as he rubbed his thumb against the top of her hand. "So I'm just sorry."

Jessica stared at their hands for a moment, slowly catching her breath. "Why are you doing that?" she asked quietly.

"I just . . . I just don't want you to hate me." The second the words were out of his mouth, Will knew he'd said the wrong thing.

Jessica yanked her hand away and let out a short, bitter laugh. "Go back to your girlfriend, Will." She lifted her chin slightly, fresh tears coursing down her cheeks. "And leave me alone." Then she turned and rushed up the hill, leaving Will with only the sensation of her touch burned into his trembling palm.

Elizabeth Wakefield

I ripped up that <u>Mademoiselle</u> quiz today. It was totally useless. I should have known better than to look to a fashion magazine for worthwhile advice. Although I did keep the rest of it for the tips on using mascara.

But actually, maybe I'm being unfair. Maybe the quiz did teach me something. That yes, I definitely am in love with the wrong guy (which I'm pretty sure I knew before buying the magazine). But also—maybe the only way to get over something is to just get over it.

Get Used to Being 12 Alone

"Jessica? Can I come in?"

Elizabeth knocked lightly on Jessica's door. All she heard were muffled sobs. At least Jessica was here. When she hadn't shown at the pep rally, Elizabeth had left the school in a panic. She knew how important this night was to Jessica, and only a major mess up could have kept her away.

There was no answer, so Elizabeth gently pushed open the door. Jessica was sitting in the middle of her bed, wearing her cheerleading uniform. Her legs were crossed Indian style and she was hunched over, clutching a white pillow to her chest. She was sobbing uncontrollably.

"Jess! What happened?" Elizabeth asked. She sat down next to her sister and started to gently rub Jessica's back. "Are you all right?"

Jessica shook her head. "They set me up," she said between gasps. "I know it sounds stupid, but they did. And now I missed the pep rally and Laufeld's probably going to throw me off the team."

"Melissa?" Elizabeth's brow knitted as she tried to make sense of Jessica's explanation.

"All of them," Jessica said, glancing up with her bloodshot eyes. "They must have all known about it. They told me the wrong place and time and I just . . . I just believed them."

Elizabeth's heart twisted, and tears sprang to her own eyes. She'd never seen Jessica so beaten and defeated. "Jess," she said tentatively, "maybe if you just explain—"

"Explain what?" Jessica blurted. "That everyone hates me? That I was stupid enough to trust them? No matter what I say, I'm telling on my teammates, and then they'll just hate me even more."

"You have to tell your coach what they did," Elizabeth said. "It's not your fault. You shouldn't get kicked off the team for it."

Jessica laughed bitterly. "You would say that."

"What's that supposed to mean?" Elizabeth asked.

"You always think everything's going to be all happy," Jessica said. "Like doing the right thing ever got anybody anywhere."

Elizabeth fought the urge to defend herself. "So, what do you want to do?"

Jessica sighed and shrugged. "I don't know. I guess I'll just lie. Tell her I had, like, food poisoning or something."

"Do you think she'll buy that?" Elizabeth asked.

"Who knows?" Jessica flopped back on her bed

and sniffled. "Who cares?" she added in a whisper.

Elizabeth lay down on her stomach next to Jessica and propped her chin up in her hands. "You know what you need to do?"

"Please! No more advice!" Jessica said, throwing both arms over her eyes. "This whole pep-rally thing was your idea, remember?"

"I know," Elizabeth said. "And I'm really sorry, but this is a very simple thing. I think you need to come hang out with me and my friends—tomorrow night. Forget the cheerleaders."

Jessica shook her head. "I'm never going out in public again."

"We both know that's not true," Elizabeth said, nudging Jessica with her elbow. "Come on, Jess. I'm talking about hanging with the good guys. Once you see that not everyone at the school is on Melissa's side, you'll feel better."

"You think?" Jessica asked, staring up at the ceiling.

"I *know*," Elizabeth said. "We'll go to the Riot, we'll dance, we'll party, and you won't think about Melissa once."

"*That* sounds like a plan," Jessica said.

"Good." Elizabeth sat up and pushed herself off the bed. "Right now I'm going to go downstairs, root through Mr. Fowler's video collection, and raid the refrigerator." Elizabeth turned to look at her sister. Jessica's face was just starting to un-blotch. "Any requests?" Elizabeth asked.

Jessica sat up, grabbed the remote, and turned on the VCR. "Nothing weepy," she said. "And get me some chocolate."

Elizabeth laughed. "No problem."

"Hey, Liz?" Jessica said as Elizabeth opened the door.

"Yeah?"

"Thanks for coming over," Jessica said.

"Anytime," Elizabeth answered.

Jessica stopped in the doorway to her parents' room as she was on her way out on Sunday evening.

"What do you think?"

Mrs. Wakefield glanced up from her magazine and smiled. "Wow! You look great, honey!" Jessica executed a little turn to show off her knee-length black dress and low-heeled silver sandals. Her hair was held off her face with two glittering combs.

"Thanks, Mom." Jessica beamed. It had been so long since she'd actually felt good about her appearance—about *anything*, for that matter.

"Where are you going tonight?" Mrs. Wakefield asked.

"I'm actually going out with Liz and some of her friends," Jessica said, leaning against the door frame.

"Really?" Mrs. Wakefield laid her magazine aside. "That's great."

"Yeah, well, we haven't seen each other that much since she moved out, and I haven't even met the people she's hanging out with," Jessica said. "I'm pretty psyched, actually."

"Good," Mrs. Wakefield said. She stood up and hugged Jessica. "I'm glad you're perking up a bit."

"Me too," Jessica said sincerely as she turned to go.

"Have fun, honey. And don't stay out too late."

"I will and I won't," Jessica promised.

She kissed her mother on the cheek, then hurried out to the Jeep.

On the way to the Riot her excitement began to turn into a major case of stage fright. She'd only been to the place once, and it had been a hellish five minutes. What if Melissa and her friends were there? What if everyone started in on her?

"Hey, this is supposed to be a good time, remember?" she muttered. She was going to walk in and find Elizabeth, and everything would be fine.

She pulled into a space in the packed parking lot, repeating the comforting words to herself. *Find Elizabeth and everything will be fine.*

The place was already jumping. Jessica squinted through the smoke and flashing lights, trying to get a glimpse of the tables. A little crowd of gossipers moved out of her way, and she spotted Elizabeth's hair. She was at a table near the dance floor, and she was whispering to someone Jessica couldn't make out in the darkness. She made a beeline for her sister, taking care to keep her eyes off the crowd.

Just as she was about to reach the table,

Elizabeth and her friend looked up. Jessica felt the smile she had plastered on her face give way.

"Tia?" Jessica said. The word was carried away on the driving beat all around her.

"Hey, Jess!" Elizabeth shouted, all smiles.

Jessica glared at Tia. "I guess you didn't expect to see me here," she said angrily. Elizabeth's face fell.

Tia tried to speak. "Well, I—"

"Did you forget to tell my sister that you tried to get me thrown off the squad?" Jessica demanded.

Elizabeth stared at Jessica in shock. "Wait a minute—"

"No, Jessica," Tia said. "You don't understand."

"Oh, don't I?" Jessica demanded. "So you didn't feed me the wrong information about the pep rally?"

Tia hesitated for a split second. It was enough to put Jessica over the edge.

"Good job, Liz," Jessica snapped. "You really introduced me to some of the good guys."

Elizabeth tried to grab Jessica's wrist as she stormed from the Riot, but Jessica slapped it away. She didn't want to hear it. And she definitely didn't want to spend the whole night with the biggest back stabber of them all.

As she strode toward her car, she didn't look back. It was time to get used to being alone. She couldn't even trust Elizabeth anymore. And if she didn't have that, she didn't have anything.

CONNER MCDERMOTT
12:37 A.M.

Elizabeth just came home, slammed the door to her room, picked up the phone, and slammed it down again. I wonder what she's so freaked out about. I can't believe she stayed out this late on a school night.

I can't believe I care.

ELIZABETH WAKEFIELD
12:40 A.M.

Would you believe that Lila won't even go get Jessica on the phone for me?

Would you believe Jessica actually thinks Tia was the one who set her up?

Would you believe she wouldn't even look at me at the Riot?

What's going on around here?

TIA RAMIREZ

12:50 A.M.

I CAN'T SLEEP. I'M TOO GUILT RIDDEN. I DIDN'T REALLY DO ANYTHING WRONG, BUT I DIDN'T DO ANYTHING RIGHT EITHER.

THAT ENDS NOW.